IF WISHES WERE HORSES

IF WISHES
WERE HORSES

by

MARION P. STROUD

VICTORY PRESS

LONDON and EASTBOURNE

SBN 85476 011 3

Printed in Great Britain for
VICTORY PRESS (Evangelical Publishers Ltd.),
Lottbridge Drove, Eastbourne, Sussex,
by Richard Clay (The Chaucer Press), Ltd.,
Bungay, Suffolk

CONTENTS

Chapter One	The Holidays Begin	*page* 7
Two	If Wishes were Horses	15
Three	Only a Shilling	22
Four	The Picnic Ride	30
Five	Opening the Door	36
Six	Hunters Ride	42
Seven	The New Kennel Maids	51
Eight	Lessons for Jake	57
Nine	The Seekers Club	61
Ten	The Day of the Show	66
Eleven	A Disastrous Morning	76
Twelve	A Needle in a Haystack	81
Thirteen	The Seekers to the Rescue	89
Fourteen	Wishes Come True	98

THE HOLIDAYS BEGIN

Patience skidded round the corner from Westhaven High Street and careered madly down Harbour Lane, pedalling furiously and swerving from side to side as she tried to avoid the pot-holes that pitted its surface. Her copper-coloured plaits bounced on her shoulders as she screeched to a halt outside Mulberry Cottage. Throwing her bicycle against the hedge, she ran up the path and round the side of the house to the open back door.

"Hello, Sally!" she panted. "I'm sorry I'm late, but I had hundreds of jobs to do before I could come out this morning."

Sally looked up from the sandwiches she was making and grinned.

"Don't worry!" she replied. "I haven't finished getting lunch ready yet, so you're just in time to help. Mummy is down at the studio today and Justin has gone off to camp with Simon Wallenger, so I thought we'd have a picnic."

"Super," said Patience. "It's very hot outside already, so it's just the day for lunch on the beach."

"I thought we might go over to the island," said Sally. "The tide is just right today."

"Better still." Patience hopped from one foot to the other. "I'm longing to see this island of yours!

Let's get the lunch done quickly." She seized the basket and began to pack the food into it at top speed.

"Hang on a sec; we're not quite ready! Your name should be Impatience," teased Sally, stacking the piles of food in her usual methodical way.

Sally never seemed to hurry, and her straight fair hair, which hung smoothly to her shoulders, was rarely ruffled. She was small for her eleven years, and, with her round face and blue eyes, she made a complete contrast to Patience, who never walked if she could run, and was tall and slim, with red hair that swung in two plaits almost to her waist.

At last, to her friend's heartfelt relief, Sally announced that she was ready, and a few moments later they were pedalling their laden bicycles down the lane. It was cool in the shade of the trees but, as they came out of the lane on to the quayside, the little village of Westhaven lay basking in the July sunshine. Out in the bay, gaily coloured yachts seemed to dance on the sparkling blue water, and behind the cobbled quay, where the High Street wound its way up the hill, the brightly painted houses and shops looked as if they might tumble into the harbour at any minute.

Sally and Patience bumped across the quay and leaned their bicycles against the white-washed boathouse that adjoined the harbour wall.

"That's Mummy's studio," said Sally, pointing up at the large windows which occupied the upper part of the boathouse and took in the whole sweep of the bay. "And there's *Sandpiper*, our boat," she added, jumping down the stone steps on to the shingle and running across to a blue-painted dinghy which was pulled up just clear of the high tide mark.

Patience followed her, and together they pushed the boat down to the water's edge.

"Hop in!" ordered Sally, jumping neatly over the gunwale.

"Hey! Wait a moment," protested Patience, scrambling awkwardly over the side as *Sandpiper* bobbed gently in the lapping waves. "I wasn't born in a boat like you!"

Sally laughed and, fitting the oars deftly in the rowlocks, began to row towards the tiny island that lay in the middle of the bay, about a quarter of a mile from the shore.

Patience gazed around her with delight. Everything was still so new and exciting. Sally had lived in Westhaven practically all her life, but Patience had spent her first eleven years in London's East End. Then came her father's sudden, frightening illness, brought on by years of overwork at his church in the dust and fumes of that poor part of London.

"You must get away and live by the coast, Mr. Hamilton," the doctor had ordered firmly, "or I won't be answerable for the consequences." So, three months before, the family had moved to Bishopsbridge, two miles along the coast from Westhaven. There, the vicarage had sea-views and a large rambling garden and in the bracing air John Hamilton soon regained his old health and energy, while Patience and the eight-year-old twins Paul and Steven revelled in their newfound freedom.

Patience and Sally had become firm friends at

Bishopsbridge School, but the busyness of the summer term had prevented Patience from exploring her new surroundings thoroughly. Now the holidays stretched endlessly ahead and she thought happily of all the plans they had made.

"There's a little inlet on the sea-ward side," said Sally as they rounded the island, "and that's where we usually land."

A few minutes later they beached the boat and jumped ashore.

"Let's take our things up to the cottage," suggested Sally. She led the way across the rough grass that bordered the beach, and up the slope to the fisherman's stone cottage that looked out to sea from the highest point on the island. Producing a large iron key from the pocket of her shorts, she opened the heavy wooden door. It was cool and dim inside and the one large room was furnished with a large table, four chairs and a roomy cupboard.

Piling their food on the table, they quickly changed into their swimsuits and ran out into the warm sunshine again. The sea seemed breathtakingly cold in contrast to the hot sand, but both girls were quite at home in the water and were soon diving, swimming and splashing like a pair of porpoises. At last hunger pangs drove them ashore to where their towels made bright patches of scarlet and blue on the golden sand.

Collecting their lunch from the cottage, they settled down to eat it under the shade of the pine trees that sheltered the cottage on three sides. From their vantage point, they could see right across the bay to the clusters of houses and hotels on the far headland that was Bishopsbridge. Westhaven village nestled in the shelter of the other headland Pipers Point, and, as they ate, Sally pointed out the landmarks.

"This island and that big house up on Pipers Point used to belong to my grandfather," she explained. "When he died, they were left to Mummy; she and Daddy were out in India then. After Daddy was killed, we came back to Westhaven and Mummy sold the house—it was much too big and expensive to run— and bought Mulberry Cottage. The man who bought the house lives in London and rents it out to summer visitors. There's an Italian couple there at the moment who want all sorts of weird foreign food from the village shop, which of course Mrs. Goodacre doesn't keep, so they're not at all popular in the village."

"It must be horrid to think of your old family home being rented out," sympathised Patience.

"Oh, not really," replied Sally, cheerfully. "I was five and Justin was eight when Daddy died, so I can only remember living at Mulberry Cottage. Mummy is too busy with her painting to bother, so we're quite happy. We've got the island still anyway, and although it's so small it's marvellous for picnics. And we've even got Barney's Wishing Chair," she added with a grin, pointing to an outcrop of rock on the far side of the cottage. "If you sit in there and wish when the moon is full and the tide is high, legend says your wishes will come true."

Patience hugged her knees and gazed out to sea. Lucky Sally, she thought, with a well-known artist for a mother and complete freedom to come and go as she pleased. Ordinary parents were much too fussy about manners and going to bed promptly and how one spent one's time. Sally, it seemed, had everything.

"What would you wish for in Barney's Chair?" she asked, rolling on to her tummy and resting her chin on her hands.

"A dog of my own."

"Surely you could have a dog as a present," said Patience; "I meant wishing for something quite impossible."

"Well, it's quite impossible for me to have a dog," explained Sally. "They make Mummy ill. If she is near to a dog or cat for long she coughs and sneezes like anything. It's a good job you didn't bring Jake today, really, just in case she's at home when we go in for tea."

Jake was Patience's bull-terrier puppy and had been her twelfth birthday present from her Scottish grandmother. He was proving very difficult to train and Patience shuddered at the thought of bringing him the two miles from Bishopsbridge while she rode her bicycle.

"I can't take him anywhere while I'm cycling, until I can persuade him not to fight every other dog we meet on the way," she grinned ruefully. "Daddy says Jake will have to go back to the kennels unless he learns to behave better very soon."

"You'd better come across and wish for a magical change in Jake, then," laughed Sally.

"Oh, no! my wish would be for a pony of my own, or even to learn to ride properly," sighed Patience. "I've had a few rides on Uncle Bob's farm and read heaps of books, but it isn't the same as proper lessons."

"Well, it's easy enough to learn round here; there are heaps of riding schools. It's not a bit like London!" Sally looked puzzled.

"I know, and that makes it even worse," wailed Patience. "But Mummy and Daddy can't afford it, not even sometimes. I did ask if I could stop my music lessons and learn riding instead, but of course they said no, so I don't suppose I'll ever learn; and to hear Mary Wentworth and her friends going on about their ponies is just torture."

"If wishes were horses, beggars would ride—well, Patience would, anyway!" Sally jumped up and brushed the sand off her legs. "Never mind, let's find some cockles for tea."

She ran along to the cottage and emerged with a bucket in either hand. Patience followed her to the beach where the out-going tide had left shallow pools shining in the sunshine.

"Paddle along very quietly," Sally instructed Patience, "and when you see two little holes close together in the sand at the bottom of the pool, grab quickly and you should find a cockle there." As she spoke, she bent down and, plunging her hand into the sand, picked up a fat cockle shell, its two halves closed firmly together.

"Looks easy enough," said Patience; "let's see who can get the most."

An hour later she realised that she was wrong.

"I'm sure they know your footsteps and wait to be caught," she complained laughingly, comparing her meagre few with Sally's half-bucket full.

B

"You'll do better next time," consoled Sally. "We've got enough here for tea, so let's head for home now, and, if you like, I'll try and teach you to row on the way back."

CHAPTER TWO

IF WISHES WERE HORSES

The rowing lesson was great fun, but a complete failure. Patience could hardly move the two oars together, and, after she had almost lost them both overboard, Sally took one while she used the other. But it was no use! *Sandpiper* bobbed round and round in circles, and they laughed so much that Sally had to take over before they were swept back to the island again.

"We'll try again another time," she panted, "but we'll never get home today if you carry on like this!"

Once back at Mulberry Cottage, Sally and Patience cleared away the remains of their picnic and began to prepare the tea.

"Mummy's forgotten the time again!" Sally flicked a few fallen leaves from the garden table as she spoke and spread it with a gay yellow cloth.

"Never mind, she doesn't like cockles, anyway!" She went indoors to cook their catch while Patience set the table.

A few minutes later, as they were sampling the cockles in the shade of the apple tree, there was the clatter of horses' hooves and a jingle of bells in the lane outside the cottage. Patience jumped up and ran to the gate in time to see four ponies and two grey donkeys with bells on their bridles go trotting past. She watched admiringly as a dark-haired boy and

girl, obviously brother and sister, each rode and led
a pony apiece, while skilfully controlling the donkeys
trotting riderless ahead of them.

They disappeared around the bend in the lane, and
Patience walked slowly back to Sally, who was munching her way through a slab of fruit cake.

"Where do those ponies come from?" she asked,
cutting herself a slice of cake.

"They're the beach-ponies from Bishopsbridge;
haven't you seen them giving rides to the holiday-
makers?"

"I've only seen the donkeys on the beach," said
Patience. "There was an elderly man looking after
them then."

"That would be Pippa and Michael's grandfather,
Joe Goldsworthy," said Sally. "He gives donkey rides
during term-time, and then in the summer holidays
Pippa and Michael take the ponies down as well."

"Do you know them well?" breathed Patience,
enviously.

"Oh, yes," said Sally, "they live just down the lane.
I helped with the ponies last summer. It was hard
work but great fun giving rides on the beach. And
that's how I learnt to ride, going to and fro to Bishopsbridge every day."

There was silence for a moment or two and then
Patience had her Great Idea.

"Sally!" she squeaked, leaping up and nearly
knocking the table over in her excitement, "why
can't you do that again this year? Then p'raps I could
help and learn to ride too!"

"Well, I don't see why we couldn't," said Sally,

cautiously. "The only thing is, we'd have to do it regularly once we started. Still, I don't suppose you'd mind the thought of that!"

"I couldn't do it on Sundays; wouldn't be allowed to, and, anyway, there's no time, what with church services and Sunday school. But every other day ... and we're not going away on holiday, of course." Patience was galloping along the beach already, in her imagination. "When do you think we can start?"

"I'll go round and ask them later this evening," promised Sally, "and you'd better ask your parents when you get home."

"Oh! They're bound to say yes," said Patience, airily. "After all, it won't cost anything. I can let you know definitely when you come to tea on Friday."

Half an hour later she set off home, lost in a delicious day-dream. She had just reached the point in her imaginings where she had reduced Mary Wentworth and her pony-owning friends to speechless admiration in a show-jumping competition, when Jake's furious barks from the gateway made her realise that she had reached home.

The vicarage was a tall Victorian building, standing back from the road at the top of Bishops Hill. It was surrounded by trees, and the back garden, into which Patience rode with the puppy worrying and growling at her heels, was a glorious tangle of shrubbery, overgrown trees and a large lawn shaded by an ancient cedar-tree.

There was no sign of her brothers, who had been building a camp in the shrubbery when she left that morning, and a glance at her watch reminded Patience

that she had only ten minutes in which to get ready
for supper. She flung her bicycle down on to the lawn
and burst in through the kitchen door to find her
mother putting the final touches to a cheese salad.

"Sorry, I'm late, Mummy; I've had a super day; can
I help?" she said all in one breath.

Mrs. Hamilton looked up and smiled. She was
quite used to her daughter's tumultuous entries and
exits.

'I've almost finished, thank you," she said serenely.
"You've just got time to get tidied up before supper.
And, Patience," she added, looking at her daughter's
sea-stained blue shorts and sandy legs, "I think it
would be an idea to change before you come to the
table."

Patience blew her mother a kiss and ran up the
stairs two at a time. The vicarage was large and rambling, with three flights of stairs between the kitchen
and her attic bedroom, and she mounted them in
record time. Her room faced west and was full of light
from the setting sun. Kicking her sandals off, she ran
over to the window for a quick glimpse of the view
of which she never tired. Below her were the topmost
branches of the cedar-tree, and beyond the garden
were row upon row of higgledy-piggledy roofs and
streets, as Bishopsbridge straggled down the hill to
the sea which glistened purple and gold in the sunset.

The crash of the bedroom door opposite announced
that the boys were on their way downstairs, and
Patience hastily pulled off her shorts and rubbed a
towel over her legs to remove the worst of the sand.
Flinging open her wardrobe door, she pulled out a

green cotton skirt and wriggled into it with the speed born of long practice. A comb tugged through the ends of her plaits and she was ready with two minutes to spare.

The dining-room was a large, shabby room and the centre of the family's activities, with its deep settee and armchairs and a big dining-table. In the winter the dining-table was usually pulled up close to the fire, but on this glorious July evening it was set close to the open french windows.

Patience finished her supper in record time and wriggled restlessly while her parents discussed the temperamental behaviour of the church boiler. Suddenly, Mr. Hamilton looked at his watch and pushed his plate to one side. "Dear me! time has flown tonight; I shall be late for choir practice," he said, picking up his Bible from the bookcase behind his chair. "We'll have prayers now, and you boys can finish afterwards."

The twins put down their apples and Patience resigned herself to waiting yet again, before she could tell her parents about the Great Idea. At last prayers were over. Patience had not heard a word, for the whole of her mind had been concentrated on one fervent prayer—"Oh, please, God, let them say yes! Oh, please!"

There was no time for preliminaries, for her father was already collecting his books together; so, without more ado, she plunged into her carefully planned speech, her words tumbling over each other in her haste.

"So you see, I can learn to ride and it won't cost a

penny," she ended triumphantly, "so please, please, say yes!"

Her mother looked at her in amazement and shook her head.

"Darling, it's quite impossible," she said gently. "You can't learn to ride by going to and fro to West-haven. Horse-riding isn't a game, and you would have to be properly taught before you could take a horse on to the roads in safety!"

"But you say we can't afford riding lessons," argued Patience, "and Sally learnt to ride that way, honestly she did."

"Well, I'm not having you risking your neck on ponies we know nothing about," said her father firmly, "and, anyway, I don't think I want my daughter to spend her time leading ponies up and down the beach. Mummy will need your help these holidays, Patience; and, if you're still keen to learn to ride later on, then we'll see if we can find the money, somehow, to have you properly taught. But this idea is definitely out."

Patience lost her temper. "It's not fair," she stormed, tears of rage and disappointment filling her eyes. "I'm never allowed to do what everyone else does. You just don't understand about riding and I'm sure I'll never have proper lessons. Well, I'm going to learn to ride somehow, so there!" With that, she ran out of the room, slamming the door behind her, and rushed upstairs to her room, ignoring her father's command to come back and apologise for her rude-ness.

Flinging herself down on the bed, she sobbed

bitterly. Why, oh, why could not her parents see the advantages of her plan?

"I'm not going to say my prayers any more," she muttered miserably. "It just proves God doesn't answer, or Mummy and Daddy would have said yes. Well, I'm going to learn to ride, somehow, whatever they say!"

At last, worn out with emotion and the exertions of the day, she fell asleep, and she did not stir when her mother slipped into the room half an hour later.

Mrs. Hamilton gazed down at her sleeping daughter's tear-stained face and sighed. She did not mind being poor for herself, but it was very hard to have to deny Patience something that she had wanted as passionately as this. She pulled the eiderdown up over her and, as she always did over family difficulties, breathed a quiet prayer.

"Heavenly Father, help Patience to understand why this has to be," she whispered, "and if there is any way in which we can let her learn to ride, please show us." She slipped silently away, confident from long years of experience that her prayer had been heard and would be answered.

CHAPTER THREE

ONLY A SHILLING

On Friday afternoon, Sally bumped down the vicarage drive on her bicycle to find Patience energetically beating rugs under the cedar-tree.

"Spring-cleaning?" she asked.

"Sort of." Patience gave the last rug a final shake and collapsed on to it, fanning herself vigorously.

"A friend of Mummy's is coming to stay tomorrow, so we're doing the guest-room out for her. She's a missionary nurse who's been ill, and she's staying for about a month to convalesce."

"What fun, having a real, live missionary in the house!" said Sally.

"Mmm!" Patience sounded doubtful. "She must be quite old, if she trained with Mummy, so she might be rather stuffy. Anyway, we'll soon know." She jumped up. "Mummy needs some bread for tea, so I said we'd go and get it. Hang on a moment and I'll go and fetch my bike."

Bishopsbridge High Street was thronged with summer visitors as Patience and Sally edged their way through the traffic to the Cake Kitchen. They collected Mrs. Hamilton's bread and then wended their way through the Arcade to their favourite shop. Favershams combined an excellent stock of saddlery and riding clothes, with a fascinating display of china and leather dogs and horses and books on every aspect of stable and kennel management.

"Why is everything to do with riding so expensive?" sighed Patience, pressing her nose against the window and gazing longingly at the beautifully tailored pair of buff jodhpurs in front of her.

"Talking of riding,"—Sally scuffed the toe of her sandal awkwardly on the pavement—"Pippa and Michael have friends coming to stay for most of the summer holidays. and so they won't want our help with the ponies after all."

"Oh well." Patience moved from the shop window reluctantly. "Mummy and Daddy wouldn't let me do it, anyway; they said it wasn't safe. But I've made up my mind—I'm going to find a way to learn to ride, somehow."

They turned and began to retrace their steps to their bicycles.

"Ugh! Look who's coming! Mary Wentworth and Julia Delaney," groaned Patience. As she spoke, Mary and Julia drew level with them and stopped. Mary smiled in the rather superior fashion that always made Patience so cross.

"Been to Favershams?" she asked. "We're just going to order our new riding jackets ready for the show next month. A bit of a bore, but still!" She turned to Sally. "Are you coming on the picnic ride next Saturday?" she asked.

Sally hesitated. "Well ... I'm not sure ... Patience will be spending the day with me, and we might want to do something else," she said lamely.

"Something else?" queried Julia, incredulously.

"Don't tell me you don't ride, Patience! I thought everybody did round here."

"But our 'Patience on a monument' isn't everybody," said Mary, sweetly; "she's the vicar's daughter!"

Patience took a deep breath. "Of course we're coming," she said, glaring at Mary; "we just hadn't discussed it, that's all. Must be going now. See you later."

She dragged Sally off down the Arcade before she could protest. As soon as she had regained her breath, Sally turned to Patience with an exasperated sigh. "You are a juggins, Patience. You know we're not going really. Now Mary and Julia will never let us hear the last of it," she said.

"Would you be going if I could?" asked Patience.

Sally hesitated. "Well," she said reluctantly, "I probably would. Judd's—that's the riding school I go to sometimes—organise these picnic rides two or three times in the summer holidays, and they're always great fun. But it doesn't matter, Patience, honestly!"

"Oh, yes, it does!" Patience had a determined glint in her eye. "I'm going if it's the last thing I do, so you go ahead and arrange it. But don't mention it to Mummy and Daddy this afternoon; I'll wait for just the right moment."

"It costs ten shillings for the afternoon," warned Sally.

"I'm sure that I've got that much in my piggy bank, and, if I can pay for myself, Mummy and Daddy can't object. Yippee!" Patience jumped on to her bicycle in great excitement and pedalled down the High

Street at a dangerous pace, while Sally followed as quickly as she dared.

The "right moment" for asking her parents did not arise that day, and the next day was gone in a flash in the bustle and excitement of their visitor's arrival. To her surprise, Patience found that Gillian was far from stuffy, and, apart from a yellowish tinge on her skin from the jaundice, not at all ill.

After supper she went upstairs to help with Gillian's unpacking. The cases were soon dealt with, and there remained only an odd-shaped parcel and a wooden box.

"You can leave the parcel," said Gillian; "that's my guitar, and I shan't need it tonight."

Patience's look of surprise was so comical that Gillian laughed. "Don't you think missionaries should have things like that?" she asked. "It's very useful, you know, in places where I work. Although I spend lots of my time nursing in the mission hospital, I also go out to the surrounding villages to tell the people about the Lord Jesus and His love for them. I've only got to sit down and start to play and sing, and I've soon got a crowd around me."

Patience digested this in silence and then pointed to the box. "Do you want to open that?"

"There's a small gift for each of you in there." Gillian undid the padlock as she spoke. "You can help me to unpack them, and tell me if you think they'll be all right."

The bed was soon covered with paper and brightly coloured oriental silk. There was a silk dressing-gown for her mother, an illustrated book on Malaysian life and customs for her father and toys for the twins. Gillian delved into the box once more and then hesitated. "I brought you a pair of embroidered Chinese slippers, originally," she said, "but your mother tells me that you are very fond of horses, so I wondered if you would prefer this." As she spoke, she unwrapped a delicately carved, little ivory horse that seemed to prance on its ebony stand.

Patience gasped. Like it? It was the most perfect thing she had ever seen. "Oh, yes, please!" she breathed, taking it gently from Gillian's outstretched hand. "I'd love it."

Gillian smiled. "I've called him Pegasus," she said, "because he looks as if he's about to fly, but you can change his name of course."

Patience shook her head. "Pegasus is just right for him," she agreed. "Thanks a million; I'll keep him for ever."

The days sped by, as the summer holidays always do, and as Patience was curled up in bed on Wednesday evening she suddenly realised that she had only two more days before the riding picnic in which to get her parents' permission. The trouble was that her piggy bank held only eight shillings and five pence halfpenny, and so she could not offer to pay for it all herself. She received her pocket money at the beginning of each month, and, as her father was very keen on 'Making money do' and 'Living within your means', there was no hope of an advance.

"What shall I do, Pegasus?" she said to the little horse prancing gaily on her bedside table, as she counted the money yet again. "I just can't bear it if they say no, and I'm sure they will if I haven't got enough money." Then a thought struck her. Why tell them? Her parents were going to London for the day on Saturday and had already given permission for her to spend the day with Sally.

"I could go first and ask afterwards," she thought, "and even if they were cross, it would be too late to *do* anything." Patience stifled the knowledge that this was being deceitful. Her mind was made up. Now to find one shilling and sixpence half-penny!

A thorough search through pockets and drawers yielded fivepence half-penny, and a penny found in the airing cupboard brought the total up to nine shillings. "Perhaps Mummy will have some jobs she wants done tomorrow," thought Patience, optimistically; "a shilling should be easy to earn", and she firmly stifled another twinge of conscience as she snuggled down to sleep.

But Thursday and Friday passed by without any jobs being offered. Patience tentatively asked her mother if there was anything extra she could do, but, when the answer was no, she did not like to press the point in case questions were asked.

Saturday dawned bright and sunny and Patience bounced out of bed, mingled anxiety and excitement fluttering like butterflies in her tummy.

She almost blurted the whole problem out at the breakfast table, but the thought of the spiteful comments from Mary and Julia, if she didn't appear on the ride, stopped her just in time.

As she was clearing the table her mother appeared in her London clothes, looking worried.

"Patience, dear, I forgot to collect the church flowers yesterday," she said. "Could you go along to Templars now and get them before you leave for Westhaven? Then Gillian can arrange them for me. They are ordered and paid for."

"Yes, of course, and I can give Jake a walk at the same time," said Patience, glad of an excuse to leave the washing-up. Templars was only a few minutes' walk away, but Jake's idea of a walk was a mad dash as he barked defiance at every dog, cat or motor-bicycle that he met on the way. Patience arrived at the flower shop quite breathless, leaving a trail of dis-approving shoppers in her wake. Fortunately, the shop was empty, and the assistant came across with the flowers immediately.

"Tell your mother, dear," she said, "that the 'four dozen mixed' worked out at less than we thought, and there is a shilling change."

Patience accepted the flowers and the shilling in numbed silence. Was this the solution to her problem? She could borrow the shilling, and her mother would not even miss it; but, on the other hand, it was not hers to spend. "But it's only a shilling, and I would pay it back, of course," she argued with herself. "I'm sure Mummy would rather lend me a shilling than let me borrow it from Sally; doesn't matter if she doesn't know that she is lending it, surely! I know! If she is still there when I get home I'll ask her, and if she's not ... well, I can't ask her, can I? And I've *got* to go on this ride! I've simply *got to*."

When Patience arrived at the vicarage, to her secret relief her parents had already left for the station.

Shutting her ears to the voice inside her that told her not to do it, Patience set off for Westhaven with her precious ten shillings safely in her purse. She was quite determined to enjoy the day to the full, whatever happened afterwards.

CHAPTER FOUR

THE PICNIC RIDE

The stableyard was a hive of activity as Patience and Sally paused at the gates of Judd's Riding School. Patience was almost bursting with excitement as she gazed round the cobbled yard. Loose boxes formed three sides of the square, and the tack room and feed stores were on either side of the gateway. Some of the ponies were already saddled and tied by their halter ropes to rings in the stable wall. Others, however, were being saddled very expertly by children who looked even younger than Sally and Patience.

Patience plucked at Sally's sleeve as she led the way to Mr. Judd's office, under the stable clock.

"Will we have to saddle our own ponies? I hope not 'cos I haven't a clue how to do it," she whispered urgently.

"Don't worry," said Sally, comfortingly. "I've told them you are a beginner, so you will have someone to show you."

She pushed open the office door and Patience followed her in. Mr. Judd, a small, weatherbeaten man dressed in an open-necked blue shirt, riding breeches and polished knee-boots, was talking to a tall, pretty girl with dark curls and a cheerful smile.

"That's Sue, the chief riding instructress," whispered Sally, as they waited quietly for the conversation to finish.

"And what can I do for you, Sally?" asked Mr. Judd, turning towards them with a smile.

"We've come to check in for the picnic ride. This is Patience Hamilton, she has not done much riding before and here's our money," said Sally, all in one breath.

"Glad to have you both." Mr. Judd ticked off their names on the list that was on his desk. "You're riding Merrylegs today, Sally," he said, "and your friend will have Greensleeves. Take your tea and put it in the van—I'm bringing that over later—and then go and find Sue. She'll fix you up!"

Their tea was quickly disposed of, and Sally and Patience went in search of Sue who was in one of the loose boxes, giving a chestnut pony a final rub with a wisp of straw.

"Sally, you can saddle Merrylegs yourself, can't you?" she asked, glancing up as they peered over the stable door. "His tack is on his peg in the tack room —that's the fifth from the left inside the door—and I've finished grooming him for you so he's all ready. If your friend—Patience, isn't it?—comes with me, I'll help her with Greensleeves."

Patience followed Sue down the row of stalls, until they came to a small grey pony, who whickered softly and pricked her ears as they approached.

"How much do you know about riding?" asked Sue, as she picked up the saddle that was propped up against the stable door.

"Not much," admitted Patience. "I've read lots of books and ridden a few times on my uncle's farm. That was two years ago, though. But I'm dying to learn."

"We'll start at the beginning, then, with saddling," said Sue. "You'd better watch me today, as we haven't much time, and then you can try yourself another time." She lifted the saddle as she spoke and flung it on to the pony's back, high up, almost on her mane. "The saddle goes up on the pony's withers—that's what we call her shoulders—and then it's drawn down on to her back, so that all the hairs lie flat and smooth and the saddle is comfortable. Then you do up the girths, and slide your fingers underneath to make sure they're not too tight and there are no wrinkles which could make the pony very sore."

Patience watched, fascinated, as Sue deftly put on the bridle, explaining what she was doing all the time. Patience was allowed to lead Greensleeves out into the yard, and Sue helped her to mount.

"Remember this rhyme: —

> *Your head and your heart you keep up;*
> *Your hands and your heels you keep down.*
> *Your knees in close to your horse's sides,*
> *And your elbows close to your own!"*

said Sue with a grin. "You won't go far wrong then."

She left Patience sitting on Greensleeves while she led a beautiful chestnut mare out of a nearby loose-box.

"This is Copper," she said, swinging easily up into the saddle. Picking up the leading rein that dangled from Greensleeves' bridle, Sue led the way over to the gates where the rest of the ride were paired off two by two. Patience saw that Sally was riding with one of their school friends, Cathryn Maners. Of Julia and Mary there was no sign.

"How many people come on the ride?" Patience asked Sue, as they clattered down the lane that led to the stables and out on to the main road.

"There are sixteen of us starting from the riding school, and then people like Julia Delaney and Steven O'Donovan, who have their own ponies, join us as we pass their homes."

Patience was longing to ask many more questions, but the ponies quickened their pace and she found she needed all her concentration to rise and fall in the saddle in time to Greensleeves' gentle trot.

"Up down! Up down!" she muttered, almost losing count as she noticed Julia and Mary join the head of the cavalcade on rather nervous-looking black ponies. She was just getting the rhythm right, when they slowed to a walk again. Sheila, the other instructress, who was leading the ride, turned off the main road and up a steep and narrow lane. Up and up it wound its way, until, with a final twist and a steep bank, they reached the downs.

The ponies all champed at their bits and flicked their tails, longing to be off over the springy turf. Sheila waited until the last stragglers had caught up, then whoosh! off they went. Greensleeves was just as excited as the others, and Patience grasped the saddle for support as the little grey mare tried valiantly to keep up with Copper's longer stride.

Sue put a steadying hand on her shoulder and suddenly Patience found she could relax and enjoy this wonderful sensation of speed and freedom. The wind blew her plaits out behind her, the sun shone warm on her face and she laughed aloud with sheer excitement. All too soon, it seemed to her, the canter slackened to a trot and then to a walk as the path wound its way through a small wood. Then, out into the sunshine of the downs again and they had arrived at the picnic place.

Mr. Judd and the riding school van had already arrived and the food was being unloaded as Patience slid to the ground on to legs that felt decidedly wobbly. The ponies were unsaddled and tethered in the shade and their riders settled down to tea.

After tea, Sheila and Sue divided the group into three according to their riding ability. While some, like Sally and Cathryn, practised riding without reins and stirrups with Sheila, Mr. Judd built some low jumps for the more experienced riders. Patience and three other beginners went with Sue, and mounted, dismounted, walked, trotted and walked again until they began to give quite a creditable performance. The afternoon ended with some mounted games which Patience was quite thankful to sit and watch, and by the time they clattered back into the stable-yard she felt as if she had never been so blissfully happy or so utterly weary in the whole of her life.

"I'd better go straight home; it's getting late," she told Sally, glancing at her watch as she lifted her bicycle from the rack. "Thanks a million for arranging such a marvellous day. It's the nicest thing I've ever done."

It was past eight o'clock when she pushed open the

kitchen door of the vicarage, to find Gillian washing up the supper dishes.

"Hello! Had a good day? The twins have had their supper and are on their way to bed," said Gillian, swishing the dirty water down the sink and pulling a wry face at the thumps and bangs that were coming from the direction of the twins' room.

"I've kept ours; I thought we'd have it in peace."

"Thanks, I'm starving! I'll just wash my hands." Patience climbed up the stairs rather more slowly than usual. The evening was oppressively hot and thundery and the excitement of the day drained way, leaving her feeling flat and tired.

Gillian had set their supper on a low table in front of the dining-room window and Patience sniffed hungrily as she saw the plump brown sausages and golden chips on her plate.

"Tuck in!" Gillian helped herself from the serving dish and sat down. "I'll tell you all my adventures when we've fed the inner man."

CHAPTER FIVE

OPENING THE DOOR

"Well?" Patience scraped the last vestige of rasp-berries and sugar from her dish and sat back with a contented sigh. "What's happened to you today?"

"I took the twins shopping in town and lost them in the Wild West Amusement Arcade," twinkled Gillian.

"The little horrors," gasped Patience, "they know they're not supposed to go in there! Mummy and Daddy would have a fit!"

"And then this afternoon," continued Gillian, "I met Mrs. Lucking."

"Oh no!" Patience pretended to tear her hair. Mrs. Lucking was the church caretaker, and was known in the family as the 'Poor old Soul' because she was always telling mournful stories. "How did she catch you?"

"Your mother left in such a rush she forgot to tell me where the church key is kept, and I wanted to do the flowers. I phoned Sally's home, so that I could ask you, but of course you were out, so it had to be Mrs. Lucking! How did the picnic ride go?"

The picnic ride! Patience's heart sank like a stone and she felt herself flushing scarlet. Of course, Mrs. Astell would have told Gillian where they were; even Sally did not know she'd gone riding without per-mission.

Gillian looked at her in surprise. "Anything wrong?" she asked.

Patience gazed at the floor and felt sick and cold all over. The enormity of what she had done suddenly struck her. What would Gillian think when she knew the truth?

"Please don't mention the ride to Mummy and Daddy," she whispered, trying hard to swallow the lump in her throat. "You see I went riding without permission. I thought I would go first and tell them afterwards, in case they said no—now I've got to tell them."

"Would it help to get it off your chest to me first?" Gillian's voice was gentle and not at all shocked, and Patience found herself pouring out the whole story.

"I'd made up my mind not to tell them after all, but to put the shilling back in Mummy's purse as soon as I could," she ended with a rush, "which just shows how awful I am. But I know I must tell them really, and it will upset them that I could be so naughty. Daddy isn't so much angry, as sad, and that makes it even worse; and they'll say I mustn't go again, and I'll just die if that happens, I really will!" With that she burst into tears.

Gillian waited until the storm had worn itself out a little, and then she spoke.

"I used to feel just the same about riding as you do," she said quietly. "My parents were happy for me to go, but I had to pay for most of my lessons myself. I used to plan and save every penny I'd got. Horses were my life and I was all set to become a riding instructress when I left school. And then, when

I was sixteen, I went to a riding camp."

"What happened then?" Patience was interested in spite of her misery.

"It was a very special sort of camp. We did lots of riding and all sorts of other horsy things during the day, and in the evening we had talks and discussions about the Bible and being a Christian. It was then that I realised, for the first time, that God really loves us and that the Lord Jesus is alive today and has a plan for each individual's life. I knew that I had been doing what *I* wanted to do, and taking no notice of Someone who loved me so much. While I was at that camp, I asked Him to come into my life, and forgive all the wrong things I'd done, and show me what *He* wanted me to do. You see I didn't come from a home like yours. You have been taught all about the Lord Jesus from the time you were tiny; it was all new to me."

"It doesn't make you any better if you have," said Patience, gloomily. "I try to be good, but it doesn't seem to work, and I keep on being naughty just the same. Praying isn't any use, either! I've prayed and prayed to be allowed to ride, and God doesn't answer."

"I think you've been putting the wrong things first," said Gillian, wisely. "We just can't be good for long on our own. There's something in our very natures —the Bible calls it sin—that always makes us want to do the wrong things. Riding is great fun, but if it —or anything else—becomes the most important thing in your life, then it's taking the place that God should have and becomes a sort of god which you worship."

Patience wriggled uncomfortably. "I've tried to read my Bible, but it's hard to understand, and God seems so far away, even though Mummy and Daddy talk about Him as if He is very near."

"But have you ever asked the Lord Jesus to help you?" asked Gillian. "He loves you so much that He died to take the punishment for all the wrong things you have ever done, even though He had done nothing wrong Himself. But He never forces Himself into people's lives. He always waits to be asked."

She picked up a book from the floor by her chair, and took out a picture postcard.

"You may have seen this before; it's called *The Light of the World*," she said, showing it to Patience. "But what is special about it?"

Patience looked at the picture for a moment and then said thoughtfully, "Well, that's the Lord Jesus standing there, and He's still wearing the crown of thorns, and has wounds in His hands and feet. He's carrying a lantern and ..." She looked again. "He's knocking at a door."

"But the special thing about the door is that there is no handle on the outside; can you see?" Gillian pointed to the door that was half-hidden by a tangle of weeds.

"That represents the door of our lives and it can only be opened from the inside—by you or me, in other words. So the Lord Jesus has to keep knocking until we will let Him in."

"But how do you know if He has come in?" asked Patience. "Do you feel very good all of a sudden?

And what happens if you ask Him and He doesn't come?"

"You've just had a birthday, haven't you?" asked Gillian.

"Yes. Why?" Patience was surprised at this change of subject.

"Did you *feel* any different when you woke up on your birthday morning?"

"Well, not really." Patience shook her head.

"Then how did you *know* that you are twelve now and not eleven?"

"I've had my birthday so I just am. That's all!"

Gillian laughed. "That's how it is with becoming a Christian! You may not feel any different, but, if you open the door to the Lord Jesus by asking Him to come into your heart and really mean it, then He will come. He has promised, you see, and He never breaks a promise. Just think! He's been knocking for twelve years; don't you think He'd be glad to come in at last?"

Gillian picked up her Bible and opened it at the last book, Revelation.

"This is the verse on which *The Light of the World* picture is based," she said, and read it aloud.

"Behold, I stand at the door, and knock: if any man hear my voice, and open the door, I will come in."

Gillian shut the Bible and looked at Patience. "It says if *any*one opens, so that means you too, but you have to do the opening."

"And would I always be good and stop wanting to go riding and all that sort of thing?" asked Patience.

Gillian smiled. "Well, it's not like a magic charm, to make you good all at once," she said. "But when the Lord Jesus has come in you're not trying alone any more, and He is always there to help you if you ask Him to. You can talk to Him at any time—that's what praying is all about—and He speaks to you as you read the Bible. As for riding, you can safely leave that to your heavenly Father. There is another verse in the Bible that says, 'All things work together for good to them that love God,' and I've proved that to be very true."

Patience was very thoughtful as she went up to bed a few moments later. She knelt by the window, looking out at the twinkling lights below her and thinking of all Gillian had said. At last, she opened her own Bible at the verse that Gillian had read, and read it again. There was the promise: "I *will* come in." And yet, would He when she had kept Him waiting for so long? Almost fearfully, she closed her eyes and whispered out the whole sad story.

"Thank you for loving me and knocking for so long, Lord Jesus," she said. "I'm sorry I've kept you waiting but please come in now and make me different because I can't be good on my own."

She opened her eyes and waited for her answer. There was no sound of a door opening, or a voice speaking in reply, and yet Patience knew in that moment that the door of her life had opened and the Light of the World had come in. She was loved and forgiven, and she breathed a prayer of thankfulness before she tumbled into bed and fell peacefully asleep.

CHAPTER SIX

HUNTERS RIDE

Bishopsbridge Station was thronged with holiday-makers, coming and going, and Patience and Sally took refuge from the crush on a luggage trolley, as they waited for the train that was bringing Justin and Simon home from camp.

"Oh! Did you hear that?" groaned Sally, as the loudspeaker boomed above their heads. "The train from London is fifteen minutes late—it *would* be!"

Patience merely grunted in reply and Sally looked at her anxiously.

"Do you feel all right?" she queried. "You've said hardly a word all morning."

Patience sighed. "I'm trying to think what to do at the moment," she confessed. "Jake has done something awful and is going to be sent back to the kennels he came from unless I can get him better trained within a month."

"Oh, no! What's happened?" asked Sally, in dismay.

"It's Mrs. Lucking," said Patience. "Jake followed me up to the church when I went to clear up the flowers on Tuesday, and while I was busy he chewed up two hassocks and a hymn book. Mrs. Lucking was cleaning at the same time, and when she found the mess he'd made she was furious."

"Oh dear!" said Sally, with a grin. "What will he

do next?"

"There's worse to follow," said Patience, gloomily. "She left before I did, and Jake chased her bike down the path—you know what he's like with bikes, and she's jolly wobbly on hers, anyway—and she fell off and sprained her ankle. Daddy was furious, because Jake bit the milkman last week, and got into a fight with Mrs. Fortescue's Dalmation the week before; so this, coming on top of Saturday, was the last straw."

"What happened on Saturday?"

"That wasn't him, that was me," said Patience. "You see, I came on the picnic ride without asking my parents, and of course they were very upset and cross when they knew. But I was truly sorry and trying hard to be different because ..." Here she hesitated and looked at Sally rather shyly. "Well, I can't explain it very well, but I've asked the Lord Jesus to come into my heart and now I'm a proper Christian. I was so happy at first, but now this has happened: I got cross with Mrs. Lucking and Daddy, and everything seems to be going wrong."

"I'm terribly sorry about Jake," said Sally, earnestly, "but it's super to know that you are a Christian too. I asked the Lord Jesus to come into my heart last Easter holidays when we had the anniversary services at Sunday school. I wanted to tell you, but somehow I didn't like to mention it before. Now, perhaps, we can help each other. There's lots of things I don't understand—about the Bible, for instance. Mummy doesn't go to church, so it's no good asking her."

"We can ask Gillian; she's marvellous at explaining things," said Patience, "but what am I going to do about Jake? Nothing I do seems to work!"

"Simon's father is a vet, so perhaps he'd know what to do," suggested Sally. "Here is the train at last, so we can soon ask Simon about it."

It took a few moments to distinguish the two boys among the hordes of passengers pouring off the London train. At last, Patience espied Simon's dark head and Justin's fair one and then they were all together, chatting and laughing, all problems temporarily forgotten.

"It's eleven o'clock." Simon glanced at the station clock as they walked through the exit. "Let's go to the Soda Fountain and I'll treat you all to knickerbocker-glories before we go home."

The other three made no objection to this splendid idea, and they were soon perched on high stools in the sea-front cafe, delving deep into their ice-cream sundaes and watching the gaily-dressed crowds strolling up and down the sunny promenade.

"Mmm, that was the best snack I've had for two weeks," said Justin, scraping the last trace of ice-cream from his glass. "Now tell us what you two have been up to while we've been away."

"You don't look very starved," remarked his sister, looking at the round sunburnt face and fair hair so like her own. "We've done lots of things, but first of all Patience needs some help."

Quickly she told the story of Jake's misdeeds and of the sentence hanging over him. "Do you think your father would know what we should do?" she asked Simon.

"Jake needs some proper obedience training, by the

sound of it," grinned Simon. "Why not take him along to the Hunters Ride?"

"The what?" queried Patience, looking quite mystified.

"It's a new boarding and training kennels that has opened up just outside Westhaven. The owners have bought old Tom Shepphard's farm, or what was left of it after he died. Dad says they are making a very good centre there."

"It would be worth going to see it anyway!" said Sally, eagerly.

"We all know you dote on anything that barks," teased Justin, "but I agree it might be a solution for Jake the Terrible."

"Let's all go tomorrow morning, then," suggested Patience. "Simon and I could come to Mulberry Cottage and we'll go on from there. I've just *got* to do something, and the sooner the better."

Tom Shepphard's old farm was perched high on the hill behind Westhaven, and the four children were quite thankful to pause for breath when they finally reached the end of the stony lane that led down to the farmhouse, the next morning.

"This is it," said Justin, pointing to the black and white painted board that was attached to the five-barred gate. "Hunters Ride Boarding and Training Kennels. Owners: Mr. and Mrs. J. Fraser. Sounds good, doesn't it? Come on, Patience; let's see what Mr. and Mrs. J. Fraser can do for Jake!"

They pushed open the gate, and walked across the yard to the low, rambling farmhouse which was built of the local sandy stone.

D

"My goodness, they've improved this," said Simon, gazing round admiringly at the crisp white paint-work and the fresh tiles on the roof. "It was really tumble-down when I saw it last."

"Looks as if someone has been whitewashing the barn and stables too." Sally pointed at the buildings which formed the second and third sides of the farm-yard square.

"Someone asking for me?"

To Sally's acute embarrassment, a lady popped her head out of one of the upstairs windows in the farm-house.

"I'm Jenny Fraser," she said. "If you hold on a moment, I'll come down."

"She must have heard everything we were saying," whispered Patience, uncomfortably.

"Doesn't matter if she did," pointed out Simon, "we were only saying nice things."

As he spoke, the farmhouse door opened and Mrs. Fraser came hurrying out. She was very small and slight with dark curly hair and sparkling green eyes. Dressed, as she was, in navy blue slacks and emerald green shirt, she looked so young and gay that Sally forgot her embarrassment at once. Within a few minutes they were all perched on stools in the cool, stone-flagged farmhouse kitchen, sipping home-made lemonade, while Patience explained why they had come.

When she had finished, Jenny Fraser sat still for a moment, looking very thoughtful.

"The trouble is, Patience," she said, "that we haven't got properly underway with our training scheme yet. At the moment we are boarding a few dogs while their owners are on holiday, and two others that, like Jake, have got out of hand and need a concentrated course of obedience training. Event-- ually, we hope to breed and train retrievers ourselves, but everything is in its early stages. Just to add to our difficulties, our kennel maid, Barbara, was involved in a car crash last week, and is in hospital with a broken leg. My husband has gone to interview a pos- sible replacement for her this morning. Until we've got some more help we couldn't take Jake as a boarder. Of course, living near, you could probably bring him every day—the Intensive Training Course lasts at least a fortnight—and it would be cheaper for you to do that."

Patience slid off her stool in dismay. She had for- gotten all about paying for the training.

"Um, er ... how much does it cost?" she faltered unhappily.

"We charge between four and six guineas a week for the boarders, depending on their size—large dogs eat more—and how badly behaved they are," laughed Mrs. Fraser. "We haven't had any day-visitors yet, but I should think the charge would be about five shillings an hour for a dog that came with its handler."

Patience nearly cried with disappointment. Since the picnic ride she was quite penniless, and she felt quite unable to ask her parents for more money after all that had happened. "I'm sorry we've bothered you," she said sadly; "I'm afraid even five shillings an hour would be too expensive for me at the moment."

Mrs. Fraser smiled at her sympathetically. "It does

add up to a lot, I know," she said, "but discuss it with
your parents, anyway; and, if you change your mind,
let us know and we'll see if we can work something
out."

They trooped out into the sunshine again, rather
subdued by this hindrance to their plans. As they
crossed the farmyard, Sally suddenly stopped and
turned to Mrs. Fraser who was walking with them to
the gate. "I've got an idea," she said, rather hesitantly.
"I've always wanted to help in a kennels—I love dogs
and can't have one of my own—so could Patience and
I come and help here in return for Jake's lessons?"

Mrs. Fraser shook her head regretfully. "I'm sorry,
Sally," she said gently, "but there's more to being a
kennel maid than liking dogs, and in any case my
husband has probably got a replacement for Barbara
by now. Do come and see us, though, any time you're
free."

She waved goodbye, and the four children set off
for home.

"Cheer up, Patience," said Simon, consolingly, as
they parted at Mulberry Cottage. "We'll think of
something. I'll ask Dad at lunch if he can give us any
tips so that we can reform Jake ourselves—it can't be
that difficult!"

"You don't know Jake!" said Patience, gloomily;
"he's as stubborn as a mule. Thanks for the thought,
anyway. We'll have to see what we can do."

As soon as lunch was over, she armed herself with
an old book that she had found on her father's shelves,
called *The Care and Training of your Dog*. Then,
having removed Jake from the vegetable garden,

where he was busy burying a bone, Patience started on his education. It was uphill work. Jake was not in the least interested in learning to sit or walk to heel, and after ten minutes he wound his lead round Patience's legs and tripped her up. She landed with an almighty thump, face downwards in a rose bed, dropping the book and scratching her elbows and knees. Jake took advantage of the diversion and disappeared into the shrubbery before Patience could pick herself up.

"You horrible animal!" wailed Patience. "If you get banished back to the kennels it's your own fault, so there!" She retrieved the book and went slowly back towards the house to wash her wounds.

"You look as if you've been in a fight!" called Gillian from her seat under the cedar-tree.

"I have!" Patience flopped down on to the grass by her deckchair, and before long was pouring out the events of the morning.

"Why is everything going wrong?" she asked. "I was so happy and good, somehow, when I first asked the Lord Jesus to come into my heart, but now I feel just as cross as I used to before. I almost wonder if I imagined it all!"

"Patience, don't let me ever hear you say that again," said Gillian, firmly. "What was the promise?"

"I *will* come in," said Patience, "and I know He did, really, but why don't I still feel the same?"

"We can't go by our feelings," said Gillian; "they just go up and down, as you know very well. We have to rely on God's promises. Have you read your Bible today?"

Patience wriggled uncomfortably. "Well, no, only

at family prayers with everyone else," she admitted. "It's so hard to understand when I read it alone."

Gillian picked up her writing case from the grass beside her chair and took out a little booklet. "These are the Scripture Union Notes for your age-group," she said. "You are given just a few verses to read each day and there's an explanation of the hard parts. But the most important thing is to find just a few words to remember all through the day—a promise, a command or a warning. This is the way in which we hear the Lord Jesus talking to us and know that He is near."

Patience looked at the booklet with interest. "I'd like to do that," she said.

"At our church in Malaysia, the boys and girls of about your age belong to the Seekers Club," said Gillian. "They promise to read the Bible every day, and they call those special few words their password. When they meet, they challenge each other for their passwords, and woe betide anyone who has forgotten it!"

"What fun!" Patience's eyes sparkled. "Could Sally and I be Seekers, do you think? She finds it hard to understand her Bible, too."

"Certainly." Gillian hunted through her writing case. "I think I've got another set of notes somewhere. You can be the first English branch of the Seekers Club; and, next time Sally comes to tea, I'll tell you both all about it."

CHAPTER SEVEN

THE NEW KENNEL MAIDS

Patience was drying the breakfast dishes when the telephone rang the next morning. Her father answered it, and then, a few minutes later, called Patience into his study.

"Mr. Wallenger has just rung up," he said.

"Simon's father? Was it with a message for me?" asked Patience.

"Mmm, in a way." Mr. Hamilton perched himself on the edge of his desk and waved towards the deep leather armchair in the corner. "Sit down, Patience, and tell me about your visit to these kennels yesterday."

"Oh!" Patience tugged at the ends of her plaits, uncomfortably. "Well, I didn't mention it because it would cost five shillings an hour for Jake to be trained there. I haven't got any money and he's my dog, so I didn't want to ask you to pay. Don't suppose we could afford it, anyway."

"Five shillings an hour for at least a fortnight would certainly mount up," agreed her father. "But Dick Wallenger seemed to think that you and Sally would like to help at the kennels in return for Jake's lessons."

"Oh yes! We'd love to, but Mrs. Fraser said no when Sally suggested it."

"It seems that they've changed their minds," said her father. "Mr. Fraser has not been able to find a suitable replacement for Barbara, and so they're willing to give you two girls a try. Wait a minute, though," he said hurriedly, as Patience leapt up with a shriek of delight. "I shall have to discuss it with Mummy first, and then go and meet these people myself."

"Oh dearest angel Daddy, please say yes," implored Patience. "You'll like them, I know you will, and I'd love to do it."

"We'll have to wait and see," said her father, trying unsuccessfully to hide the twinkle in his eye. "I'll visit them this afternoon and we'll talk about it again at tea."

That afternoon seemed the longest that Patience had ever known. She prowled restlessly to and fro, unable to settle to anything, and eventually telephoned Sally, who, when she heard the news, was wildly excited.

"Mummy will say yes if your father does, I know," she said breathlessly. "We'll just have to pray very hard that he likes the Frasers."

"Gillian says that we should pray that things will be decided the way God wants them to be," said Patience, thoughtfully, "because then, whatever happens, we can be sure it's the right way. So I'm trying very hard to do that—but I still hope and hope and hope that Daddy says yes," she ended with a chuckle.

"Let me know as soon as you do," instructed Sally. "I'll stay by the phone all evening, till you ring."

She did not have to wait for long. As soon as tea was over Patience dashed to the telephone. "It's all right, Sally," she gasped, almost speechless with excitement. "My parents have said yes, and Daddy is going to contact your mother this evening. If it's all right with her, we're to go along tomorrow afternoon and be shown what to do, and then after that take Jake there every morning except Sundays. After his lessons, we're to stay on and help till lunch time. Isn't it marvellous? I'll see you tomorrow."

Prompt at 2 o'clock, Patience and Sally arrived at Hunters Ride. This time they made their way straight to the farmhouse door and, before they could knock, it was flung open by a smiling Mrs. Fraser.

"The two new kennel maids!" she exclaimed. "You *are* a welcome sight. Come in and have a cool drink after that long cycle ride, and we can have a chat at the same time."

The girls followed her down the passage to the kitchen. "That's Tishoo, the other member of the family," said Mrs. Fraser, pointing to a beautiful marmalade cat, who was sunning himself on the window-sill. "When you've had your drinks we'll go and find my husband. He's down at the kennels at the moment. By the way, if you are working with us, we'd like you to call us Jock and Jinny—it's friendlier."

They sipped their delicious home-made lemonade as Jinny explained the kennel routine, and then followed her out of the kitchen door and across the back courtyard to the Dutch barn behind the farmhouse. The open-sided barn covered the dog's sleeping quarters and their wire-mesh runs projected out on either side of the kennels so that part of the run was under cover and part outside. Beyond the barn and its neighbouring two fields, was the bracken and cliff grass of the headland and then the sparkling blue sea.

"What a super place to work," exclaimed Patience. "You've got a view right across the bay and I suppose that's Sally's ancestral home over to the right there on Pipers Point."

As she spoke, the door of the end run clanged shut and a tall, fair-haired man with a rather thin, lined face came towards them, limping slightly as he walked.

"Meet our new kennel maids, darling!" called his wife. "Patience and Sally, this is Jock!"

The girls greeted him shyly, rather overawed by his quiet manner which was such a contrast to his wife's sparkling gaiety. He soon went to his office while Jinny showed them round the kennels and the old dairy adjoining the barn, which was used for food preparation.

"It's just like a big kitchen," said Sally, looking at the long bench table, large cooker, sink and refrigerator. Jinny showed them the cupboards holding biscuits and baked brown bread, and the shelves of doggy dishes.

Jock's office was next to the dairy and beyond that was a small room where the dogs were groomed.

"And that's just about it, at the moment," said Jinny. "The barn opposite the stables is used as an indoor training school for the early stages of the Obedience Training and if it's wet. The stables are empty still, except for Shadow and Shubelle."

"Who are they?" queried Patience.

"Oh, they are horses," replied Jinny, "or at least Shubelle is my own horse, and Shadow a rather elderly pony that we saved from slaughter last year."

She noticed Patience's skip of excitement and smiled. "I'll introduce you to them later on; they're out at grass just at the moment," she said. "We're hoping to have a pony-trekking centre here one day. We'll probably have guests staying in the house and riding out to a different beauty-spot each day, as well as local people coming for day treks. That will be my side of things. Jock wants to breed and train retrievers and take dogs for specialised Obedience Training. You see, before his accident he used to train police dogs."

"What a marvellous idea," enthused Patience.

"How many dogs have you here at the moment?" asked Sally.

"Our own pair of retrievers, Lady and Crusader," said Jinny, leading the way back to the kennels. "Then two 'Obedience' boarders. Judge is a black Labrador and Buccaneer is an Alsation. We've had them for a month so they will be leaving us soon. We have four ordinary holiday boarders, and, of course, Mrs. Fotherington-Jones' famous Cherie. Have you heard of her?"

Sally and Patience shook their heads.

"She's a very valuable poodle and insured for goodness knows how much," Jinny told them. "We feel quite honoured to have her while Mrs. Fotherington-Jones is in America, especially as we are going to show her in the County Agricultural Show next month. Whatever you do, while you're working here, don't make any mistakes with Cherie!"

Sally and Patience shuddered at the thought and

made up their minds that they would have as little to do with Cherie as possible.

"Not that anything could happen to her," thought Patience as, later, they helped the Frasers to take all the dogs for a glorious romp over the headland. "But I want to go on helping at this super place, so I'm not taking any chances."

CHAPTER EIGHT

LESSONS FOR JAKE

Patience was dreading Jake's first lesson after his mis-behaviour at home, and hoped that she would have time to take him for a walk beforehand to work off some of his high spirits. But Jinny met them at the gates the next day with a cheerful "Morning girls! Sally, will you come down to the kennels with me, please? Patience, Jock is waiting for you in the train-ing barn."

Before she had time to get nervous, Patience found herself in the barn, chatting to Jock while he made a fuss of Jake.

To her surprise, the lessons started with instruc-tions for her, while Jake was allowed to explore the exciting smells in the barn.

"Both you and Jake have to learn together," ex-plained Jock, "and you must be clear in your own mind what you're trying to achieve, then plug away until you achieve it. Jake has had his own way for nine months so he won't give in easily; but a well-trained dog is a happy dog, so it's worth persevering. Bull-terriers are very strong dogs," he went on, "so, as we do with all the working dogs, we shall use a choke chain with his lead instead of an ordinary collar."

As he spoke, Jock showed Patience a loop of loose chain links, which he slipped over Jake's head, removing his leather collar as he did so. "This is loose, but not so loose that it will slip over his ears. If you do have to pull on the lead to emphasise a command, the chain tightens for a second and brings the point home."

While Patience examined Jake's new collar, Jock left the barn and re-appeared with Lady, the golden retriever. "I'll demonstrate how things should be done," he said with a smile, "and then we'll try with Jake."

Patience tethered Jake and perched herself on a bale of straw, watching wide-eyed while Lady performed faultlessly.

Jock held her lead in his right hand, and kept the dog on his left side. "Then I have my left hand free for encouragement or correction," he explained to Patience. Lady sat, and stayed sitting while Jock walked away from her, then came bounding to him as soon as he called. She walked to heel, keeping her shoulder level with Jock's knee no matter how swiftly he changed direction, and finally dropped to the floor like a stone at Jock's ringing command, "Down".

"She's marvellous," enthused Patience, giving Lady a well-deserved pat, "but Jake will never be like that, I'm sure!"

"Of course he will if you're prepared to work!" said Jock, bracingly. "You demonstrate what you want done, repeat it till he catches on, and then reward him with lots of praise. Simple, really! We'll start to teach him to 'sit' and 'walk to heel' today—he won't take everything in at once."

Patience found the next half hour exhausting, but,

sure enough, by the end of the lesson, Jake would 'sit' with only a gentle reminding pressure from her left hand on his hindquarters, and he kept reasonably close to Patience as she walked briskly up and down the barn.

"Well done!" Jock looked at his watch. "We'll leave it for now, or Jake will get bored with the whole procedure. Bring him in again, just before lunchtime, and go through everything again for ten minutes or so. Later on today, spend another ten minutes reminding him of it. Demonstration, repetition and reward—they are the key-words. Take yourself off to the kitchen for a drink now, and I'll put Jake in a spare run across in the kennels until you're ready for him again."

Patience thanked him and hurried off, glad to be able to relax for a moment. In the kitchen she found Sally pouring out some lemonade, while deep in conversation with the elderly lady who was energetically scrubbing the floor.

"This is Mrs. Bones, who helps in the house, Patience," introduced Sally. "Mrs. Bones—my friend, Patience Hamilton."

"Please to meet you, miss, I'm sure," nodded Mrs. Bones, scrubbing relentlessly on. "You'll be a great help to Mr. and Mrs. Fraser, after Barbara's accident and all. Not but what they didn't need more than the one girl, anyway, with all there is to do, and Mr. Fraser not much better than lame."

"What's the matter with his leg?" queried Patience. "I hardly liked to ask him."

"No secret about that!" Mrs. Bones sat back on her

heels and pushed her sleeves up a little higher. "He had a car crash, swerving to miss a dog as had darted into the road, and a child after it. It's a wonder he lived, so they say, but of course he lost his right leg. Got a false one below the knee, you know!"

"Really?" said Sally, wide-eyed. "No wonder he's so keen on obedience training."

"Er, Sally ..." Patience could foresee these fascinating revelations going on all day. "What does Jinny want us to do now?"

"Crumbs!" Sally looked at her watch and downed the rest of the lemonade in a hurry. "We've got to cut up the meat for today's feeds first, and then exercise the holiday boarders, so we'd better get a move on!"

The rest of the morning flew past and Patience was delighted to find that Jake's second lesson was a considerable improvement on the first. His progress continued throughout the week, and Patience and Sally settled happily into the kennels' routine, soon feeling as if they had been working there for years.

Jinny quickly discovered that Patience loved horses; and, to her great delight, Patience was given Shadow to groom as one of her special jobs.

"I may not be learning to ride," she confided to Sally, "but at least I'll know how to look after a horse, which is a step in the right direction!"

Sally nodded. "It's the same for me," she agreed. "I feel as if I've got a share in all the dogs here, but especially Judge—and he seems to like me. I hope Jake doesn't reform too quickly—I want to go on working here for ever."

CHAPTER NINE

THE SEEKERS CLUB

Patience and Sally had been helping at Hunters Ride for almost a fortnight when the schedules for the County Agricultural Show arrived. Jock and Jinny called them both into the office where the entry forms and details were spread all over the desk.

"How would you like to enter for the show, girls?" asked Jinny, handing them the schedules.

"What as? Fat cattle?" grinned Patience, peering over Sally's shoulder as she read through the Agricultural Classes.

"You'd be a dead loss for that unless we could feed you up a bit," said Sally, rudely.

"Well! I like that! I eat just as much as you do," began Patience, when Jock interrupted with a firm, "It's the Dog Show Section that we're concentrating on mainly. Look, Patience, there is a 'Novice Obedience, Dog handled by Child under Fourteen'. I think Jake might manage that in another fortnight or so."

Patience gave a shriek of excitement.

"Sally could enter Judge for that too—I've got permission from his owners. It's all good advertising for us, and practice for you both."

"What about you?" asked Sally.

"I shall take Crusader and Lady in for the Open Obedience and their Breed Classes, and Jinny will show Cherie for Mrs. Fotherington-Jones."

"I might try Shubelle in the Handy Hunter and Jumping too, if I can find time for some practice," added Jinny.

"Looks as if we'll be busy," said Patience. "I should love to try Jake if you think he's good enough. Just think what my parents would say if he won!" She tailed off into happy day-dream, until she was rudely awakened by Jock's reminder that, unless she got on with his training, Jake would undoubtedly be bottom of his class.

For the rest of the week, they were all hard at work, practising, exercising, feeding and practising again.

"I feel as if I'm living 'Dog Show' at the moment," said Sally as they left the kennels on Friday.

"I know, I haven't seen Justin or Simon for ages," agreed Patience.

"Oh, they're sailing-mad now and preparing for the Regatta which comes just after the Agricultural Show," said Sally, "but they did suggest a picnic over on the island tomorrow afternoon."

"Super! Oh dear ..." Patience stopped. "I did tell Gillian that I would ask you to tea tomorrow so that she could explain all about the Seekers Club—remember I told you about it ages ago?"

"Yes, and I'd love to know about it, but I've half promised the boys! I know, why not ask Gillian to our picnic—she's well enough for that sort of thing now, isn't she. And she's not at all like an ordinary grown-up!"

Patience nodded vigorously. "But what about Justin

and Simon?" she asked. "They won't want to hear about it, will they?"

"Oh yes! I think they would be interested too," said Sally. "You see, I've been meaning to tell you—the most marvellous thing has happened. Justin and Simon's camp was one like Gillian went to, only theirs was for sailing, and Justin asked the Lord Jesus into his heart while he was there. He told me all about it last Sunday after church. Simon has been a Christian for a long time, so perhaps we could all be Seekers."

"That would be fun," agreed Patience. "If Gillian is agreeable, we'll meet you down at the boathouse at three o'clock tomorrow, then."

The next afternoon was ideal for a picnic—hot and sunny with a slight off-shore breeze.

"The wind is just right for us to sail over to the island and it's easier than rowing," said Simon, stowing the food into his father's sailing dinghy, *Flying Fish*.

"Sally and I will race you three, if you like," suggested Justin, "*Sandpiper* only takes two, really, and it would be good practice."

"Certainly, if you don't mind being beaten," replied Simon, airily.

A challenge like this was not to be ignored, and after a hasty, "Ready, Set, Go", the crews pushed off and set sail for the island with all speed. *Flying Fish* was the larger boat, but Simon's crew were inexperienced and Justin and Sally had taken a boat across to the island innumerable times. As they rounded the island, *Sandpiper* was a little behind, but a sharp tack brought the two boats level and their keels grated on the beach together.

"Phew! That was a jolly good race," said Simon, peeling off his shirt. "Now what I need is a swim."

This was a treat still denied to Gillian, so the four left her to unpack the picnic basket and light a fire for tea while they splashed and dived in the sunlit water.

The smell of sausages frying brought them out of the water at last, and they were soon hungrily munching the sausages that they spiked from the pan with pieces of driftwood and sandwiched in crisp new rolls.

"Mmm! Give me hot-dogs rather than sandwiches, any day," said Patience, starting on her third sausage and second packet of potato crisps.

"Yes, something cooked out of doors always tastes nicer," agreed Gillian, pushing some scrubbed potatoes into the embers of the fire to bake, and cutting a fruit cake into thick slices. "We do a lot of cooking like this abroad."

"Could you tell us about the Seekers while we're eating tea?" asked Sally.

"Certainly!" Gillian helped herself to some food and leant back against a boulder. "It was started for boys and girls who were real Christians—I think you all know what I mean." There were shy nods all round, and she continued: "It was intended to help them understand the Bible. We chose the name 'Seekers' because, as the rules say, 'You seek to know the Lord Jesus as a real Saviour and Friend; you seek to understand the Bible and you seek to tell others about Him.' Seekers promise to read the Bible every day and find a password from it—that's a message to help them, of no more than five words, so that they can remember it and tell other members if they are challenged."

"The trouble is the Bible is so hard to understand, that I don't know where to start," said Justin.

"I find it hard to keep up with reading it every day," admitted Simon.

"These booklets will help with both those difficulties," said Gillian, showing them the notes that she had given to Patience. "They give you just a few verses to read and explain the hard parts. Having something definite to do helps you to keep it up too."

"Can we all have the notes?" asked Sally.

"Yes, certainly, and the badges that go with them," said Gillian, producing four small badges. "As you can see, there's a gold lamp on a green background. The lamp represents the Bible which gives us light as we seek, so, although it's the Scripture Union badge, which is given to the readers of these notes, we've made it the Seekers' badge too. If you'll each promise to obey the Seekers' rules, which are written on this card, I'll give you your badges now."

One by one the four solemnly read out the rules and promised to obey them, and, as they did so, Gillian gave them their badges.

"From tomorrow onwards, I shall challenge you for your password every time we meet," laughed Gillian. "Woe betide you if I catch you out—you'll have to buy me an ice-cream, and of course I'll do the same for you. And now I declare the first English branch of the Seekers Club to be well and truly formed."

CHAPTER TEN

THE DAY OF THE SHOW

The day of the Show dawned fine, with only a slight breeze to stir the wisps of sea-mist that clung to the trees around Mulberry Cottage. Patience, who had spent the night with Sally, awoke without the help of the alarm clock that they had set so carefully the night before and sat up in bed.

"Sally, are you awake?" she hissed, peering at the clock in the half-light. "It's half-past five, so we might as well get up."

The mound of bedclothes that was Sally stirred slightly.

"Come on!" Patience bounced out of bed and gave her friend a shake. "There's heaps to do, so it's no good snoring. I'll go and wash, and I'll bring a damp sponge back with me so you'd better be up!" With a rush of bare feet she was gone.

Sally uncurled and pushed her feet out of bed, yawning and stretching as she did so. By the time Patience came pattering back, however, both beds were made and Sally was curled up in the chair by the window, her Bible open on her knee.

"Oh dear! I nearly forgot about passwords this morning," said Patience, pulling on her navy jeans and sweater, and plaiting her hair with the speed born of long practice.

"Let's do our reading together," suggested Sally,

"then we're both sure to have a password, when we see the others at the Show."

For the next ten minutes Sally and Patience tried to fix their minds on the day's reading from the fifteenth chapter of St. John's Gospel. The reading over, they chose their passwords.

"I'm going to have 'love one another' from verse seventeen," said Patience. "I get cross with people so easily, that's just the reminder I need."

"Yes, I thought of that one," nodded Sally, "but I think I'll have verse fourteen. 'You are my friends' —that makes the Lord Jesus seem very near, and reminds me that I must behave like His friend too."

For a moment they slid on their knees and asked God to bless this most exciting of days, and then Patience whirled downstairs to get the breakfast.

An hour later, they were bumping down the lane leading to Hunters Ride. Jock and Jinny were already hard at work brushing the dogs and cleaning up the kennels. Without more ado, Sally got to work on her beloved Judge, while Patience put the finishing touches to Jake who had stayed at the kennels overnight. By nine o'clock Shubelle was loaded into the horsebox, the dogs and their equipment were all securely in the kennels' van, and, with the arrival of Jock's brother who was to look after the rest of the dogs for the day, the Hunters Ride entry set off for the Show.

The showground was already busy when they arrived, with horseboxes and cattletrucks bumping slowly over the grass, and riders exercising their shining ponies up and down the field. The sun was shining brightly from a cloudless sky and the flags on the top of the marquees and the judges stand fluttered bravely in the breeze. Patience and Sally let the dogs out of the van and breathed the mingled smells of horses and trampled grass with great enjoyment.

"Give the hounds a quick run round the field," instructed Jock, as he went off to the secretary's tent for their competition numbers, "and then bring them over to the Dog Show Marquee to be benched. And, whatever you do, Patience, hang on to Cherie. We don't want to lose her in this crowd."

Patience shuddered at the thought and tightened her hold on Cherie's lead. The exercising was accomplished without any hitches, however, and, once the dogs were all comfortably settled on their respective benches, Patience and Sally were free to enjoy themselves until their events in the afternoon.

"I think I'll stay here," said Sally, looking at the programme. "I want to see how Lady and Crusader do in their classes, and Cherie too."

"Let's see," said Patience; "Jinny and Shubelle will be in the ring for the Ladies Hack Class in a few minutes, so I'll go and watch that. See you later."

The morning passed in a flash and proved to be a very successful one for the Hunters Ride entries. Shubelle and Jinny were placed third in their class, and Patience returned to the Dog Show Marquee to find Sally proudly pinning first prize certificates and red rosettes on the bench beside Crusader and Cherie.

"Isn't it super?" said Sally, waving towards her handiwork. "That means we've got two silver cups as well to collect at the prizewinners' parade, and Lady got the reserve in the Sporting Dog or Bitch Class."

"Jinny must be relieved that Cherie won," said Patience, patting the little black poodle affectionately. "Mrs. Fotherington-Jones would have been furious if she hadn't."

"Seems to me that's all she cares about," said Sally. "Poor Cherie—she is not a dog, she is a gold-mine. She won the Open Class too, you know, for all breeds of dogs, as well as the poodle section. And guess what?"

Patience shook her head.

"Mary Wentworth won the Alsatian Class with her father's dog Saracen."

"Goodness, I would have thought dog shows were beneath her," said Patience. "Anyway, I hope she's not in our Obedience Class—I'd hate her to beat me!"

They refilled the water bowl, and were just about to take their picnic lunch out under the trees, when a swarthy-faced lady and gentleman stopped by Cherie's side.

"This is the little dog that won two prizes," said the lady to her companion, her voice marked by a strong foreign accent. "She is beautiful, no? I will give her a prize too."

Sally and Patience were standing on the other side of the row of benches, and, before they could stop her, she had given Cherie a large chocolate biscuit.

"Go and get Jock or Jinny quickly," hissed Sally to Patience, squeezing her way through the crowds to get to Cherie's bench.

"Excuse me, but you mustn't feed the dogs," she said firmly, just as the lady was about to offer a second biscuit.

"What business is it of yours, little girl?" asked the gentleman, with a scowl.

Sally bristled. "I work for the kennels where Cherie is staying," she replied coldly, "and she must never have tit-bits like this."

"I am Mrs. Montanelli from Westhaven House," announced the lady, as if that settled the matter. "I wish to buy the dog. Take me to her owner."

"I'm afraid that's impossible; she's in America," said Sally, trying hard to be polite to this odd couple. To her relief she saw Jock pushing his way towards her, and thankfully left the problem to him.

The Montanellis repeated their request to buy Cherie and asked Jock to cable the message to her owner.

"I must have this dog," said Mrs. Montanelli, with a pout. "I will visit you next week to hear the reply."

Jock promised to do what they wanted, and ushered them firmly to the tent exit. "I'll sit with the dogs while you have your lunch," he told the girls, grimly. "The Mrs. Montanellis of this world are a menace."

"Do you think she'll really buy Cherie?" queried Patience.

"No, I expect she'll have forgotten about it by tea-time," Jock replied, "but I'll stay with the dogs all the same. Off you go!"

Patience and Sally went over and joined Jinny, who was sitting by the horsebox in the shade of the trees, and between mouthfuls told her what had happened.

"We'll have to keep someone near the dogs all the

time," said Jinny, "but let's not worry now—you've got to keep your mind on your classes this afternoon."

"Puts me off my food, to think of that," groaned Patience; "I'm sure Jake will forget everything I've ever taught him!"

"Nonsense!" said Jinny, briskly, biting into a juicy apple and giving the core to Shubelle. "Are your parents coming to see him perform?"

"Oh, yes! The whole family is turning up, and even Justin and Simon are taking an afternoon off from sailing in honour of the event."

"What about your mother, Sally?" Jinny queried.

Sally pulled a face. "Great-aunt Emma is coming to stay for her summer holidays, today," she said, "so Mummy has to meet her train. The trouble is Aunt Emma often forgets what train she's coming on, so meeting her can take hours. Last year she changed her mind at the last minute and came by bus a day later!"

"Never mind, you'll have Justin to cheer for you if your mother doesn't arrive," consoled Patience, jumping to her feet and collecting up the remains of her lunch. "Come on, Sally; we'd better give the dogs a quick run and then get changed. See you later, Jinny!"

Their class was the first of the afternoon's events and attracted a large crowd of spectators. With fast-beating hearts, Patience and Sally joined the other competitors in the collecting ring and looked around at the opposition.

There were two other Labradors beside Judge, Bess, a Border Collie belonging to Jane Wheatley, one of their school-friends, a poodle, several smaller dogs and Mary Wentworth with the Alsatian, Saracen. Patience pulled a gloomy face at Sally who shrugged her shoulders resignedly. A moment later, the bell rang and the roar of the spectators' conversation became a buzz as one by one the handlers led their dogs into the ring. In single file they walked around twice, and Patience breathed a prayer of thankfulness as she realised that, far from being upset by the crowds and the other dogs, Jake was on his best behaviour and seemed to be enjoying himself. He walked quietly to heel, and, as soon as the order came to stop, sat down promptly without being told. After the preliminaries, the ring was cleared and the dogs re-entered one at a time to do their individual tests.

Sally was first, and, although she was quaking inwardly, she went through the test, apparently as calm as ever. Judge trotted round the ring at her heels, sat on command, and stayed still while she dropped his lead and walked away across the ring. So convinced was he that he must sit still, Judge spoiled an otherwise perfect performance by having to be called twice. The judges awarded him ninety marks and Sally left the ring to a generous round of applause.

The next few competitors were not so successful, and Patience started her turn with only Judge's marks to beat. It was certainly Jake's day. With eyes bright and tail aquiver, he performed the exercises as if he had never misbehaved in his life. All the same, Patience could hardly believe her eyes when the thunderous applause and the score-card on the judges table told her that Jake had earned one hundred marks the highest possible score.

Hardly daring to breathe, her heart thumping with excitement, Patience watched the rest of Jake's rivals perform one by one. To her amazement, none of them gained full marks. At last, there was only one more dog left to compete—Saracen, and with him Mary Wentworth.

"Why on earth is Mary over here? She should be riding today," muttered Patience to herself, watching with a sinking heart as Saracen went faultlessly through the exercises. "It's very odd."

But, odd or not, Saracen had also collected full marks; Patience had tied with the successful Mary in a competition.

The judges called them both back into the ring and examined the dogs closely. Patience held her breath, trying to ignore Mary at her side, while the judge looked from Jake to Saracen and back again. Finally, he cleared his throat.

"Did you train this dog yourself?" he asked Patience.

"Yes, I did, when I'd been shown how to do it." She was surprised to find that her voice sounded quite calm.

"And you?" He looked at Mary. There was a heart-stopping pause and then she shook her head.

"No," she admitted, "my father did most of it."

"I see."

The judge gave the red rosette to Patience. "In that case, I think Jake is the winner, because in this competition the handler can gain marks too. Saracen is a very close second. Well done, all of you!"

There was a burst of applause and then the Border

Collie, Bess, was called in third, followed by Sally and Judge, who collected the reserve.

Once out of the ring, Sally and Patience did a war-dance of joy.

"I knew Jake had it in him," exulted Patience. "Good old Judge, too!"

Out of the corner of her eye she suddenly saw Mary standing rather disconsolately by herself. Patience felt tempted to rush past her to the family who were waiting to add their congratulations, and then her password came unbidden to her mind. "Love one another". She stopped.

"I'm sorry we couldn't both win, Mary," she said rather awkwardly, "but jolly good, anyway. I expect you will collect some firsts in the riding, instead."

To her horror, Patience saw tears glinting in Mary's eyes.

"No," Mary said with a sniff, "I'm not riding to-day. I haven't done very well at shows lately, and Daddy hasn't any time for failures, so my cousin Sandra is riding Firefly instead. If he doesn't win with a different rider, he's going to be sold."

Patience was quite horrified. How awful to have parents like that! To think she had often envied Mary her pony and her exciting life at her father's hotel!

"Are you here all alone, then?" she asked.

Mary nodded. "I can't bear to watch anyone else riding Firefly, so I think I'll go home," she said sadly.

Patience hesitated. Mary had been very unkind to her once or twice in the past, but loving people meant forgiving them too. She held out her hand.

"Come and have tea with us first," she said; "my

parents would love to meet you and Saracen and I
... well, I'd like you to come too."

Mary looked disbelieving. "Are you sure?" she
asked. "We ... well, I haven't been too nice to you in
the past; do you really want me to?"

"I really do," said Patience, who was surprised to
find she meant it. "Come on, let's find Jane and Sally
and I'll buy you all a celebration ice."

CHAPTER ELEVEN

A DISASTROUS MORNING

The next two or three days seemed very dull after all the excitement of the Show. Jock's brother, Sam, was staying at Hunters Ride and so Sally and Patience were given a holiday.

"I thought I'd enjoy having a few lazy mornings," confided Patience to her mother, "but I really miss all the dogs and grooming dear old Shadow. There doesn't seem much else to do!"

"Of course, you could sort out some of your drawers and sew a few buttons on here and there," suggested Mrs. Hamilton, with a twinkle; "there's only a fortnight before school starts."

"What a gruesome thought," shuddered Patience. "Come to think of it, I ought to go shopping for Daddy's birthday present this morning, and tomorrow we'll be helping Jock and Jinny again, so I haven't got time for sewing! What a pity! But I'd do your shopping for you, Mummy darling!" and before her mother could have any more brilliant ideas she darted away.

Sally and Patience arrived at Hunters Ride the next morning to find Jinny looking rather harassed.

"Thank goodness you've come," she called as they wheeled their bicycles across the farmyard. "Jock has taken Sam and his family down to the station, and then he's going to collect a couple of new holiday boarders, so I'm single handed this morning. Patience, if you could see to Shadow, and Sally could start chopping up for the evening's feeds, I'd be very grateful. We've got several new boarders arriving today, so I'm getting the kennels ready."

Patience loved grooming the old grey pony and used to pretend to herself that he was her own as she brushed and rubbed at his coat until it shone. Jinny had offered to let her ride him, but after the picnic ride her parents had forbidden any more riding during these holidays, so Patience contented herself with learning stable management as a first step.

"One day, though," she told Shadow, "you and I will go trotting down the lane, you'll see." The pony pushed his nose against her affectionately and then lifted his head as Jinny appeared at the stable door.

"Patience," she said, a frown on her usually cheerful face, "a client has just rung up from Salters Bay to ask if we can collect his dog before midday today. He has to go abroad at a moment's notice. Jock won't be back in time to go, I know, so do you think that you and Sally could hold the fort here for an hour while I go and get the dog? I've finished the exercising and everything is quiet."

"Of course," said Patience, readily, "we can manage. I'll get an extra kennel ready while I'm doing the others."

"Thanks a million." Jinny's brow cleared. "I shan't be long. Can you tell Sally? and I'll dash off straight away."

Patience felt very pleased with life as she rechecked that all the dogs were safely in their runs, and then

F

went indoors to find Sally pouring out their lemonade.

Sally grinned as she heard the news. "I've always wanted to be in charge," she said, puffing out her chest; "now, slave, hurry up and get the kennels ready while I recline in the sun."

Patience pulled a horrible face and was about to pounce on her, when the sound of a car coming into the farmyard made her dash to the window, instead.

"Jock's back early," she began, and then stopped. "Sally!" she hissed, "just look at who's arrived: that ghastly Montanelli woman!"

"Oh, no!" Sally joined her at the window and watched with horror as the plump Mrs. Montanelli climbed out of the car, followed by the tall, dark-haired young woman who had been driving. "Well, she can't eat us," said Sally, resolutely squaring her shoulders, "so let's go and see what she wants."

As she spoke, there was a loud hammering on the front door, and the sound of Mrs. Bones' voice as she answered it. They hurried down the hall.

"Mr. and Mrs. Fraser are out, so we'll help these ladies, thank you, Mrs. Bones," said Patience, firmly, seeing that Mrs. Bones was about to launch into one of her long and involved explanations.

"Out?" Mrs. Montanelli's chest swelled indignantly. "But I wish to see them particularly!"

"I'm very sorry," said Sally, politely. "Would you like to come back this afternoon?"

"I will not," said Mrs. Montanelli, "be bumped down that execrable lane again. I will await their return."

"Perhaps they could call on you," suggested Sally.

hoping to get rid of her. "Where do you live?"

"We rent Westhaven House, but, thank you, now I am here I will remain. The matter is urgent, you understand."

"I'm afraid they won't be back till lunchtime," said Patience, hastily, horrified at the thought of having this dog-feeding monster around the kennels all morning.

"Perhaps ..." Mrs. Montanelli eyed them with disfavour; "but with two children like you, I must write it down. I no longer wish for the dog, the poodle Cherie. I have bought another, even more beautiful, you see."

"Come into the office, then," suggested Sally, "and you can write a note in comfort."

To this suggestion Mrs. Montanelli grudgingly agreed, and, with a majestic, "Come, Maria!" to her companion, she followed Sally to the office.

Patience was about to join the procession, when she heard the telephone ringing in the house. She hurried in to answer it and a man's voice asked, "Is that Mrs. Fraser?"

"No," said Patience, "I'm afraid she's out."

"I'm expecting her to collect a dog of mine; how long will she be?"

Patience glanced at her watch. "She should be there by now," she said.

"Well, she's not!"

The voice at the other end sounded rather impatient. "I have to leave the house now, so my housekeeper will hand Juno over. But I'll give you his feeding instructions and routine now, if I may."

"Another fussy owner," groaned Patience to herself as she went to collect a notebook and pencil. And so he was! By the time Juno's feeding instructions had been duly noted and his routine repeated at least six times, Patience could see Maria and Mrs. Montanelli outside in the farmyard again. At last Sally ushered them into the car, and Patience was able to replace the telephone receiver.

"That's nearly half an hour we've wasted," said Sally, glancing ruefully at her watch. "We'd better get on at top speed now, or those kennels will never be ready."

The ran across to the Dutch barn, calling to the dogs as they went. They had almost reached the unoccupied kennels, when Patience stopped dead. "Sally," she gasped, "just look at Cherie's run! The gate is open and she's not inside."

"Oh! she's in the kennel asleep, I expect," said Sally, her face chalk white, despite her reassuring words. But the kennel, like the run, was empty, and Cherie was nowhere to be seen.

"She was here when I came in for a drink, I know she was!" Patience was almost sobbing with fright.

"She can't be very far away," said Sally, trying desperately to keep calm. "You go round the buildings and I'll run out on to the headland in case she's suddenly fancied a walk."

Fear lent them wings as they raced off, hunting frantically in every corner likely and unlikely, and calling and whistling until they were hoarse. But after half an hour they had to admit defeat. Cherie was nowhere to be found; she had vanished without a trace.

CHAPTER TWELVE

A NEEDLE IN A HAYSTACK

Lunch-time at Mulberry Cottage was a gloomy affair.
"I just can't understand it," said Patience, miserably,
pushing her plate of ham salad away from her, almost
untouched. "I'm sure Cherie's run was closed when I
looked, and I *think* I saw her in the kennel, and yet
she got out."

"Or was taken out," said Sally, darkly, as she ladled
trifle into the glass dishes in front of her and pushed
two across to Justin and Simon.

"Do Jock and Jinny think she's been stolen, then?"
asked Simon.

Patience shrugged. "They're phoning the police at
two o'clock if they haven't found her by then," she
replied. "I must say it seems like it, especially as that
call for Jinny turned out to be a fake. And yet who
could have taken her and why?"

"She's a jolly valuable dog and would probably fetch
a lot of money abroad," Sally pointed out, "and it
would be fairly easy for someone to come across the
headland and get at the kennels. Of course, this morning, with Jock out and Jinny off on a wild goose chase,
it was ideal."

"Why was Jinny on a wild goose chase?" queried
Justin.

"Well, she got an urgent call to collect a holiday
boarder," explained Patience, "and when she arrived

81

at the address, the house was empty. Of course, she could have mistaken the address, and in fact a man did ring again and ask where she had got to, but it seems odd."

"Very odd," agreed Simon. "Who answered the phone?"

"I did," said Patience, "and he sounded genuine enough—fussed on and on about his wretched dog all the time Sally was seeing to Mrs. Montanelli."

"So you were both busy at once. Curioser and curioser!" Simon looked very thoughtful.

"Perhaps dear Mrs. Montanelli knows something," suggested Justin.

"Oh, no! She came specially to say she doesn't want Cherie any more, and, anyway, she was with me all the time," said Sally.

"Not wanting Cherie could just have been an excuse," said Simon. "Where was Mr. Montanelli?"

"In London, or so his wife said."

"Hmm! Well, we've only got her word for that."

"We did suggest this to Jock," Patience told him, "but he pooh-poohed the idea. They think Cherie's got out somehow, and are going to have another hunt over the headland and fields this afternoon."

"Are you helping?" asked Justin.

"We can't; we've got to look after great-aunt Emma. It's 'the Mortimer Woodham day' today—remember?" said Sally. She saw Simon's puzzled frown, and laughed. "Sir Mortimer Woodham is the famous art critic and he's coming to tea with Mummy. He may sponsor an exhibition of her paintings in London," she explained. "Patience and I promised that we would take Great-aunt Emma up to the church this afternoon so that she can do some of her beloved brass rubbings and Mummy can entertain her visitor in peace. I wish we could get out of it now, though, and help Jock and Jinny look for Cherie."

"How about it, Justin? Shall we go up to Hunters Ride and help?" suggested Simon. "You girls can't break your promise, but, if you could find out a bit more about the Montanellis this afternoon, I think it might prove very interesting! Cheer up, Patience! This is another sort of seeking, but the Seekers are in action and we'll find Cherie. I think we ought to ask the Lord Jesus to help us."

The others looked rather embarrassed. None of them was used to praying in front of other people.

"Okay," said Justin, finally; "it's your idea, so you can do it."

"Righto!" Simon was not in the least put out. "No time like the present. We'll do it now, before we wash up."

They sat around the table with eyes shut, and Simon prayed aloud for them all, telling the Lord Jesus what had happened and asking for His help.

"Thank you," said Patience, when he had finished. "I'm glad you've done that. We'll find Cherie now; I just know we will."

The afternoon was hot and sunny, but, in spite of the heat, Great-aunt Emma set off on their expedition dressed in her usual navy blue coat, her black straw hat pinned firmly to her silvery curls. She had a large roll of paper tucked under her arm, and she trotted along at an amazing rate for so elderly a lady.

"I'm hot in a dress, so Great-aunt Emma must be boiling," whispered Patience to Sally as they toiled up the hill to the church. "I wonder how the search is going," she went on, thinking longingly of the cool breezes up on the headland.

"Wish we were with them," muttered Sally; "I can't help feeling that it's our fault that Cherie's gone, even though Jock and Jinny were so nice about it."

As she spoke, they reached the church and Great-aunt Emma turned to them with her vague smile. "Don't stay with me, my dears," she said; "I'm sure you would like to be outside on a lovely afternoon like this."

"Well, we have got an errand to do," said Patience, quickly, cutting short Sally's polite protests. "But we'll be back soon, and then we'd love to see your brass-rubbing. Goodbye!" She whisked up the road and Sally had to run to catch up with her.

"Where are you off to now?" panted Sally, crossly. "You know we're supposed to stay with Aunt Emma, and anyway, we haven't time to get along to the headland."

"No, but we have got time to pay a call on Mrs. Montanelli," grinned Patience. "Westhaven House is only just down the lane, isn't it?"

"What excuse have we got to do that?"

Patience pulled a key out of her pocket. "I found this in the office after our visitors had gone this morning. It doesn't belong to Jinny, so we could call and ask if it belongs to Mrs. Montanelli or Maria."

"It's worth trying," Sally sounded rather doubtful. "We won't find much out by doing that, though."

"But, don't you see? it will give us a chance to get into the house and grounds and see if there's any sign of Cherie."

Sally felt in the pocket of her skirt. "I've got my high-frequency dog-whistle here too," she said more hopefully. "I can blow this and no human can hear it, but, if Cherie does, she'll bark. I've used it with her before."

"Super," said Patience. "Let's climb over the wall and have a look round the grounds first."

"We can get through a side gate; the lock is broken," said Sally, leading the way down the lane. "It would look rather suspicious if anyone saw us climbing the wall."

The gardens were large and overgrown, and the girls had no difficulty in hiding themselves as they made their way cautiously towards the back of the house.

"The old stables and coach house are the obvious places to look," whispered Sally, as they squeezed through the tangle of bushes in the kitchen garden.

"Ssh, what's that?" Patience stopped suddenly and ducked down behind a pile of flower-pots, pulling Sally down beside her.

"Sounds like a pig grunting over the other side of that hedge." Sally pointed a shaking finger in the direction of the noise.

Cautiously, they rose to their feet and tip-toed across the garden.

"It's a pig, all right, but a human one." Patience peered through the hedge and turned an excited face to Sally. "So much for Mr. Montanelli being in

London! He's asleep in a deckchair, right there in the summerhouse. We're getting warmer. I'm sure Cherie's here somewhere."

"Dare we go on? He might wake up!" quavered Sally.

"Of course we're going on," said Patience, stoutly; "we can always say we're looking for the front of the house, if we meet anyone. Get the whistle out and let's get going."

The stableyard was quite deserted and the old coach house, which was used as a garage, empty of cars. "It looks as if they're out," said Sally, feeling much braver. She blew her whistle and they listened hard, but all they could hear was the murmur of the bees in the kitchen garden and the faint rumble of snores from the summerhouse.

"Let's get nearer to the house," suggested Patience, walking softly across the yard. Sally blew the whistle again.

"Listen!" Patience clutched her arm. "That was a whine; I know it was!"

"I heard it too, but where was it coming from?" Sally strained her ears in the direction of the sound. "I'll try the whistle once more."

"There! That was definitely a bark." Patience was scarlet with excitement. "And it seemed to come from the house, but very low down!"

"The cellars! Of course! That's where she'll be." Sally pointed to the small glass squares which were just visible in the courtyard pavings adjoining the house. "There is a warren of cellars under Westhaven House, and it would be a marvellous place to hide anything."

"Oh, help! How on earth are we going to make sure it's Cherie down there?" groaned Patience. "We can't go and knock on the door and ask for a conducted tour of the cellars and it's no good telling Jock and Jinny till we're sure."

Sally thought hard. "I know," she said at last. "There is a secret way into the cellars that Daddy used to tell us about. The smugglers used it in olden times. I can't remember much about it, but Justin came and found it once when the house was empty, so he would know. We'll ask him and then come back again."

"Tonight! That would be the best time, when everyone's asleep," decided Patience. "If they have got Cherie there, I shouldn't think they'll try and move her till all the fuss has died down. And if they haven't —well, no one will be any the wiser. Now, let's go and beard Mrs. Montanelli."

"Must we?" demurred Sally. "We've found out all we need to know, surely."

"I want to see her face when we mention that Cherie is missing," said Patience, making her way to the front of the house, "and you might get a chance to try the whistle in the house. We can see if she still says her husband is in London too. If she does, that would be very suspicious. Come on."

Patience was doomed to disappointment, however. Three long peals on the large, black bell-handle beside the front door produced no response, and she had to agree with Sally that the house was empty.

"We'll go down the front drive, anyway," said Patience. "We might meet them coming in."

But, much to Sally's relief, they left the gates of Westhaven House without meeting anyone. "Great-aunt Emma will be wondering where we are." Sally glanced at her watch and quickened her pace to a jog-trot.

"And we haven't learnt how to brass-rub," said Patience, running easily at her side.

"Perhaps she'll show us quickly, before we go," said Sally; "I'd like to go into the church for a few minutes, anyway. I know we can talk to God anywhere, but, as we're near to His house, we might as well say thank you there."

"You mean because our prayer at lunch-time is being answered," said Patience. "You know, coming up here with Great-aunt Emma has been one of the 'all things working together for good' that the Bible talks about. That is my password today, and I thought at lunch-time that it doesn't work, but now ... oh yes! we'll certainly say thank you!"

CHAPTER THIRTEEN

THE SEEKERS TO THE RESCUE

The alarm clock under her pillow buzzed loudly and Patience awoke with a jump. For a moment she lay still, wondering where she was and why she had woken in the middle of the night. Then she remembered and shivered with excitement.

"Sally!" she hissed across the bedroom. "Wake up! It's midnight and time to go."

Sally sat up in bed. "I haven't been to sleep yet," she whispered. "I've been listening for Mummy to go to bed."

"And has she?"

"Yes, about half an hour ago, but she doesn't always go to sleep straight away, so we must be very quiet."

They slid out of bed and began to dress, feeling for their clothes in the dark.

"I'm jolly glad Mummy said I could stay with you for the night, but I wish I'd got my own dog-rescuing clothes with me," groaned Patience, as she struggled into a pair of Justin's navy blue jeans and a dark school sweater of Sally's.

"Never mind; if you look a fright no one will see you," Sally consoled her, laughingly, pulling on her own dark slacks and sweater at top speed. She tiptoed towards the door. "Come on. Justin has just gone downstairs. And mind the middle two stairs; they creak!"

They were soon safely in the kitchen, drinking steaming mugs of cocoa made by Justin, and tucking into thick slabs of rich fruit cake.

"Nothing like getting up in the night to give you an appetite," grinned Justin, cutting himself another slice of cake.

"Oh, come on!" Patience was hopping restlessly from one foot to the other. "We'll never get there if you are going to sit and eat all night."

"Patience, Patience!" Justin opened the back door very quietly and switched on his torch. "Simon isn't meeting us till half-past twelve, but that's three minutes from now, so off we go! And don't forget to walk on the grass; the gravel on the drive makes an awful row!"

The moon was almost full, and the trees cast black shadows down the lane as they padded along in single file. Simon joined them as they left the lane to take the short cut across the fields, looming out of the hedge so suddenly that Sally nearly jumped out of her skin.

"Adventures like this are all very well in books and during the day-time," she whispered to Patience, "but I don't like the countryside at night. It makes noises!"

Patience gave her arm a squeeze. "It doesn't seem very friendly to me, either, but there's nothing to be afraid of really, I suppose," she whispered back. "All the same, I wish we could've brought Jake with us. Still, just think how wonderful it will be if we find Cherie. We'll be glad we came, then."

It was not long before they reached the gate to Westhaven House that Patience and Sally had used earlier, and Simon stopped with his hand on the latch.

"One of you girls had better lead the way through the gardens," he suggested, "as you've been here recently. Once we get to the stables, Justin is in charge because he knows the secret way in. And remember! no talking and no torches. We don't want to be spotted from the house."

One by one, they filed silently through the gate and Patience led the way cautiously through the tangled gardens.

"Mind the piles of plant-pots," she whispered, as they reached the kitchen garden. "They're ..." but it was too late. Even as she spoke, Justin tripped over a straggling creeper, and, as he stumbled against them, a stack of wooden boxes crashed through the empty cucumber frames. The noise sounded deafening in the silence of the night and the four shrank into the shadows, quaking with fright, their hearts pounding as they waited for Mr. Montanelli to come rushing out to investigate.

All remained quiet. After a breathless few minutes, Simon got up and tip-toed on to the path again. "I don't think they heard. I can't see any lights on," he said, "so let's carry on. And *be careful*, everyone!"

Nobody needed this warning. Patience and Sally were still trembling when they finally reached the stables and eased open the creaking door.

"I haven't been in here for ages," muttered Justin as he shone his torch carefully over the floor, "so I hope I can find the flagstone. It's in the right-hand corner, I think; look for a stone with a metal ring in the centre, and that's it."

The stable had obviously been used as a storehouse

for a long time and the floor was thick with dust.

"We'll never find a metal ring in this light," complained Sally, crawling round on her hands and knees and choking as the dust flew up in her face. "It's hopeless."

"Nonsense!" said Simon, firmly. "We've just got to be thorough, that's all! Get up, Sally, and we'll sweep the floor first with this old brush." He swept the right-hand side of the stable as well as he could with the worn old brush, and Justin and Sally examined the floor stone by stone in the light of Justin's torch.

"Are you *sure* it was the right-hand side, Justin?" asked Simon, resting back on his heels with a sigh. "There's no ring in any of these stones."

Just then, Patience, who was lifting boxes away from the back wall, gave a muffled shriek. "Justin come here quickly! I think I've found it!" Shining her torch on to the floor, she pointed to a large stone slab in front of the broken manger. Sure enough, there was a dirty metal ring embedded in the centre.

"Well done, Patience!" Justin thumped her on the back enthusiastically. "Now to get it up." He took a length of stout cord from his pocket and threaded it through the ring.

"Grab hold of it with me, Simon," he ordered, "and pull *hard*!" At first, it seemed as if even their combined efforts were going to be unsuccessful, then suddenly there was a creaking noise and the stone was lifted slowly up on end. They crowded round the open hole, and by the light of Simon's torch saw a metal ladder disappearing down into the darkness.

"We'll just tie the cord to the manger here," said Justin, deftly knotting it round a protruding nail as he spoke. "It would be very awkward if the stone fell down while we were down below!"

Sally went quite pale at the thought. "Are you *quite* sure it won't?" she asked anxiously.

"Of course, goose," said her brother, reassuringly, "and don't say you'd rather wait for us up here, because you know you'd be scared stiff all by yourself!"

Sally smiled sheepishly. "Well, if we're going, let's get going," she said bravely.

"Right! Now listen!" Justin squatted down on his heels and drew a diagram in the dust. "This ladder takes us down to a passage, and at the end of the passage is the secret cellar where the smugglers used to hide their goods. There's no door into it from the house because it's underneath the other cellars. Fortunately, the trapdoor is marked, so we won't have to look for that. And remember, once we're in the ordinary cellars, not a sound!"

Without more ado, he turned and climbed quickly down the ladder, and Sally followed. "You next, Patience," said Simon, shining his torch on to the ladder for her and then following at top speed.

The passage smelt musty and dank and Patience wondered with a shudder if there were bats swooping silently in the darkness ahead, but nothing more sinister than a cobweb touched her cheek. By the time she reached the smugglers' cellar, Justin had piled two empty boxes on top of one another and was struggling to lift the trapdoor that was marked with a white-washed cross on the low ceiling. It gave way with a

G

sudden plop, and Justin swung himself up through the hole, disappearing into the room above. With a heave from above and a push from below, the two girls followed him and, as soon as Simon had joined them, they set off to search the cellars for Cherie.

"We'll find the main passage from the kitchen," whispered Simon, "and if there are footmarks leading anywhere, we'll follow them. I don't suppose the Montanellis would use the cellars normally, so if there are any footmarks they should lead to Cherie."

The dusty passages twisted and turned in all directions and it was some time before the children found themselves in the wide main passage.

"Which way is the kitchen, do you think?" asked Patience.

"There's no sign of footmarks up that way," said Justin, shining his torch along the floor, "so we'd better go along here."

They walked along in single file, shining their torches on to the floor, but to their dismay, as the passages neared the kitchen, the floor became cleaner and there was nothing to show if anyone had been along there before them.

"Are you sure you heard a dog barking this afternoon?" asked Simon as they reached the flight of steps leading up to the kitchen.

"Of course we did!" snapped Patience. "She's here somewhere, I'm certain."

"Look! What's that?" Sally pointed to a mark on the floor nearby. "Let's try that little side passage; it looks to me as if someone has spilt water down there."

The others crowded after her as she ran down a narrow corridor which ended abruptly at a large cellar door.

"The door is bolted on the outside!" Justin's voice was hoarse with excitement. "Let's look inside."

The bolt slid back easily and the door opened on well-oiled hinges. Simon and Justin shone their torches inside.

"She's there! Look! Asleep in that corner!" cried Sally, pointing to a pile of sacks. "But why doesn't she wake up? Do you think she's dead?" With a sob Sally rushed forward and cradled the little black poodle in her arms. "Cherie, wake up! We've come to rescue you!"

Simon felt the little dog gently. "She's all right; just drugged to stop her barking, I should think," he said cheerfully. "That proves that dear Mrs. Montanelli is up to no good, and the sooner we get the police the better."

"I'll carry Cherie," said Sally, starting for the door.

"Oh, no! We'll have to leave her here till we get back, or the Montanellis could deny the whole thing," said Simon firmly.

"What?" Sally's eyes glistened. "I'm not leaving here here with those monsters. They might spirit her away again. If she stays, so do I."

"Good for you, Sally," Justin gave his sister a hug. "There's a bolt on the inside of the door, so you lock yourself in with the proof whilst we go for help. We can run faster than you; otherwise I'd offer to stay."

"I'll stay too," volunteered Patience, "and we won't open the door unless you say my today's password;

then we'll know it's you."

"Thank you, Patience!" said Sally, gratefully. "I shall feel much safer if you're here too, and we'll only open the door if we hear a voice saying, 'All things work together for good.' Goodbye, you two, and please, *please* be quick!"

They bolted the door behind Justin and Simon and settled down on the sacks with the sleeping Cherie.

"Do you think the Montanellis will try and slip away during the night with Cherie?" asked Sally, fearfully.

"No!" said Patience, sounding much braver than she felt, "and, anyway, we've locked the door on our side so they can't get in. We've got to remember that the Lord Jesus is with us and 'All things work together for good', so, although it's dark and spooky down here and I don't like it one bit, I'm jolly well *not* going to be scared!"

The minutes dragged by. Curled up side by side on the sacks, Patience and Sally were half asleep when the faint slam of a door broke the silence.

"Listen!" Sally grabbed Patience's arm. "Either the Montanellis are leaving at the crack of dawn or the others are back."

They strained their ears, hardly daring to breathe as they listened for footsteps in the passage outside.

"Don't say a word till we know who it is," breathed Patience in Sally's ear. "If it's the Montanellis, they may think the door is just stuck and go away again for a little while if we are quiet."

"Or they may try and break it down," quavered

Sally, wishing that she had not read so many adventure stories.

"Ssh, there they come; we'll soon know." Patience switched off her torch, and Sally clasped the still sleeping Cherie tightly in her arms, determined to hold on to her whatever happened.

The knock on the door was unexpectedly loud. "All things work together for good. so you can unbolt the door!" Simon and Justin chanted the password together, and with a shout of relief Patience and Sally opened the door and tumbled out of the cellar.

"Ooh! You've switched the light on!" Patience screwed up her eyes at the unaccustomed brightness, as, both talking at once, the boys led the way to the kitchen stairs.

"Is it safe to bring Cherie up now?" asked Sally, hesitating at the bottom.

"Oh, yes! There are two burly policemen upstairs, as well as Jock and Jinny, so there's nothing to be afraid of," Simon assured her, and he led the way through the rambling kitchen and sculleries to the welcome brightness of the hall.

CHAPTER FOURTEEN

WISHES COME TRUE

"I should be very cross with you, of course." Jock looked at the four weary children sitting round the table at Hunters Ride, with a twinkle in his eye. "Roaming round the countryside at night and breaking into other people's houses! Shocking behaviour!"

"We tried to tell you, but you just wouldn't listen." Sally was quite upset by his stern tone.

"Yes, and we're very grateful to you, Sally." Jinny patted her on the shoulder consolingly. "You saved the kennels by finding Cherie. If we had lost a valuable dog like her, no one else would have trusted us with their dogs, and quite rightly so."

"Did the police find out what our friends were up to?" asked Patience, taking the bowl of steaming porridge that Jinny handed to her and covering it liberally with cream and sugar.

"Sergeant Jones was still questioning Maria when we left." Jinny picked up her own plate and sat down at the end of the table. "Unfortunately, the Montanellis went off to London early yesterday evening, so we haven't caught them yet! Maria was not expecting them back until tomorrow—no, of course it's today now! Goodness, it's half past five already!"

"Maria vows that she didn't know Cherie was in the cellar until last night. Then she overheard Mr. Montanelli telling his wife how easy it had been to

98

slip across the headland and take Cherie while Maria and Mrs. Montanelli were with you," continued Jock. "Maria was very frightened and planned to slip away from Westhaven House before her employers returned, and get the first available boat back to Italy."

"But why steal Cherie at all?" asked Justin. "Is she really worth all the trouble?"

"She's a valuable dog," said Jinny, "but I think there's more to it than that. From what Maria overheard, it seems that the Montanellis were employed to steal Cherie so that her owners could claim the insurance. The dog was then to be smuggled abroad, and she could either be sold or used for breeding in another country. Her owners would then have the money from this and a large sum from the insurance company too."

"You mean Mrs. Fotherington-Jones is up to something like that?" Simon looked amazed.

"We don't know for certain, but it's possible." Jinny yawned. "Anyway, it's time that you four made up for some of your lost sleep, so finish your bacon and egg and I'll show you your bedrooms. Jock has contacted your parents and they've agreed to let you sleep off your adventures here. After that, you're going to have some explaining to do."

It was the sunshine flickering on to her face through the bedroom window that woke Sally eventually. She yawned and stretched, then gazed around the unfamiliar bedroom in bewilderment, wondering where she was. A dog barking outside brought memories of the night before flooding back, and she hopped out of bed and ran to the window. Below her were the kennels, and sure enough there was Cherie stretched out asleep in the sunshine, apparently none the worse for her adventures.

"It's true, it's true and Cherie's safe!" Sally hummed the words to herself as she dressed hastily, leaving her borrowed pyjamas on the bed. Patience's bed was already empty, and Sally ran downstairs to find the other three sitting at the kitchen table eating a belated lunch.

"Come on, sleepy-head, it's nearly three o'clock." Justin scraped up his last spoonful of apple-pie and ice-cream and leaned back in his chair with a contented sigh. "We've left you a few scrapings, but you'd better hurry up and eat them before I feel like a fourth helping!"

"Pig!" Sally pulled a face at her brother and tucked into her cold chicken and salad with a will. Soon they were all talking at once, reliving the excitement of the night before.

"Sergeant Jones wants to talk to you and Patience, Sally," said Simon as they paused for breath at last. "We have told him all we know, but he wants to hear exactly what you did and saw yesterday while you were in charge here, and during your hunt in the gardens at Westhaven House."

"And then I suppose we'll have to go home." Sally looked rather worried. "Do you think Mummy will be very cross with us, Justin?"

"I don't think so," said Justin, cheerfully. "Jock has been doing some telephoning while we've been asleep and we're not going home—straightaway that is. Jock and Jinny have invited us all to a celebration

A

barbecue, and all the grown-ups are coming too."

"Isn't it a marvellous idea?" Patience jumped up and began to clear the table at top speed. "We'll help with the dogs, Sally, while Justin and Simon collect some wood, and we'll have the biggest camp-fire that Westhaven has ever seen!"

The rest of the afternoon passed in a flash. Sally and Patience set to with a will, and finished the evening feeds and exercise in record time. Then a trestle table with a gay checked cloth was set up near the driftwood fire, and the girls rushed backwards and forwards from the kitchen with bowls of salad, rosy apples and long French loaves. Strings of sausages were carefully pricked and put in the iron frying pans, and scrubbed potatoes put around the edge of the fire to bake, while Justin and Simon arranged chairs and rugs around the fire on the springy cliff grass.

Soon, the visitors had arrived and the flames of the fire were leaping up into the velvety September dusk. Patience sniffed the mingled smells of coffee, frying sausages and wood smoke, and heaved a happy sigh. Judging from the babble of laughter and conversation, the party seemed to be going with a swing. Dreamily, she watched her parents leaning back comfortably in their deckchairs, laughing and talking to Simon's father, while Jinny and Gillian were sharing a joke with Mrs. Astell. Patience grinned as she saw Great-aunt Emma deep in conversation with Mrs. Wallenger. Simon's mother would know all about brass-rubbings before the end of the evening!

"Wake up! You're supposed to be handing those

sausages round." Simon's voice brought her back to earth with a bump and she hurriedly did as she was asked. Soon, all the plates were filled and for a moment there was silence, broken only by the distant wash of the waves on the shore, as Mr. Hamilton stood up to say grace. Then the cheerful chatter broke out again as the story of Cherie's adventures were told and retold.

At last, when every crumb of food was eaten, and Patience and Sally were handing round the mugs of steaming coffee, Jock rose to his feet.

"Ladies, gentlemen and others," he said, waving his hand towards Jake who was padding round beside Patience. "You all know that we are here to celebrate Cherie's safe return. Now some 'stop-press' news! I have just been talking to Sergeant Jones and I'm glad to say that the police have taken Mr. and Mrs. Montanelli to Bishopsbridge Station for questioning." Everybody clapped excitedly at this piece of news and, when the noise had died down, he went on: "Jinny and I want to thank Patience, Sally, Justin and Simon for finding Cherie—if she had stayed lost, the kennels would have been ruined. So, although we musn't encourage them to wander round the countryside at night, we are very thankful that they did on this occasion." At this point there was more applause and the four children squirmed with embarrassment. Jock held up his hand for silence and continued. "Not only have we to thank them for this, but we should also like to thank Sally and Patience for their cheerful help with the kennel-work while Barbara has been away. We couldn't have managed without them." He turned towards Patience and Sally and spoke directly to them. "I've been talking to your parents," he smiled, "and we have their permission to thank you in a practical way."

As he spoke, Jinny stepped forward into the fire-light, leading Judge, the black Labrador. "Sally," said Jock, with a broad smile, "Judge's owners have to go abroad unexpectedly, and they have asked us to sell him for them. We have bought him ourselves, and will keep him here if necessary, but he's yours, if you would like him for your very own." Sally took the lead that Jinny held out to her and gasped out her thanks, then fell on to her knees beside Judge, bury-ing her face in his black coat, quite speechless with joy.

Jinny handed an envelope to Patience. "This is a kind of cheque," she smiled. "It gives you sole charge of Shadow and promises one riding lesson each week all through the winter."

Patience could hardly believe her ears. She hugged the precious envelope to her, looking questioningly at her parents who nodded and smiled, while Jock gave another envelope to Justin and Simon. "We know that you are keen sailors," he said, "so buy something for your boat, and thank you all very much."

There was a storm of applause and exclamations as everyone tried to thank everyone else all at once.

When the noise died down a little, Gillian picked up her guitar, strumming softly and singing in her lilting voice. The others listened and then, one by one, joined in. The fire flickered and sank lower and Patience, curled up on the rug with Jake beside her, gazed dreamily into the fire, thinking of the exciting winter ahead.

At last, Mr. Hamilton rose reluctantly to his feet. "It's been a wonderful party," he said, with his gentle smile, "but it is ten o'clock and we must go. We've all sung ourselves hoarse, I know, but may we end with a very short favourite of mine? We have so much to thank our heavenly Father for; let's sing the Doxology."

There was a murmur of agreement before Gillian played the first chord, and then their voices rang out joyfully on the soft night air.

> *"Praise God, from whom all blessings flow;*
> *Praise Him, ye people here below;*
> *Praise Him above, ye heavenly host;*
> *Praise Father, Son, and Holy Ghost."*

Patience sighed happily and hugged Jake and her precious envelope closer. It was the perfect ending to this most exciting of summer holidays.